"What Would The Women's Council Say If They Knew We Were Spending The Night Together—Again?" Michael Asked.

Kylie's smirk died. "You know good and well that the traditions of Freedom Valley are that if a couple spends the night together, the man is expected to go before the council and present himself as a proper bridegroom candidate. It isn't necessary, but it's a custom that every woman really wants, no matter how modern she is. Our mothers and grandmothers had wanted the same, and were courted according to the custom. I can't see you doing that. You've been a Cull too long. You have all those women. You're a legend in your own time, a heartthrob of every girl when we were younger. You wouldn't do that just to embarrass me, like that kiss on the dance floor, would you?"

"Wouldn't I?"

* * *

"…Ms. London creates complex, humanly flawed characters who overcome great emotional turmoil to reach a wonderful happy ending."
—*Romantic Times Magazine*

Dear Reader,

The year 2000 has been a special time for Silhouette, as we've celebrated our 20th anniversary. Readers from all over the world have written to tell us what they love about our books, and we'd like to share with you part of a letter from Carolyn Dann of Grand Bend, Ontario, who's a fan of Silhouette Desire. Carolyn wrote, "I like the storylines...the characters...the front covers... All the characters in the books are the kind of people you like to read about. They're all down-to-earth, everyday people." And as a grand finale to our anniversary year, Silhouette Desire offers six of your favorite authors for an especially memorable month's worth of passionate, powerful, provocative reading!

We begin the lineup with the always wonderful Barbara Boswell's MAN OF THE MONTH, *Irresistible You,* in which a single woman nine months pregnant meets her perfect hero while on jury duty. The incomparable Cait London continues her exciting miniseries FREEDOM VALLEY with *Slow Fever.* Against a beautiful Montana backdrop, the oldest Bennett sister is courted by a man who spurned her in their teenage years. And *A Season for Love,* in which Sheriff Jericho Rivers regains his lost love, continues the new miniseries MEN OF BELLE TERRE by beloved author BJ James.

Don't miss the thrilling conclusion to the Desire miniseries FORTUNE'S CHILDREN: THE GROOMS in Peggy Moreland's *Groom of Fortune.* Elizabeth Bevarly will delight you with *Monahan's Gamble.* And *Expecting the Boss's Baby* is the launch title of Leanne Banks's new miniseries, MILLION DOLLAR MEN, which offers wealthy, philanthropic bachelors guaranteed to seduce you.

We hope all readers of Silhouette Desire will treasure the gift of this special month.

Happy holidays!

Joan Marlow Golan

Joan Marlow Golan
Senior Editor, Silhouette Desire

Please address questions and book requests to:
Silhouette Reader Service
U.S.: 3010 Walden Ave., P.O. Box 1325, Buffalo, NY 14269
Canadian: P.O. Box 609, Fort Erie, Ont. L2A 5X3

CAIT LONDON

SLOW FEVER

Published by Silhouette Books

America's Publisher of Contemporary Romance

 SILHOUETTE BOOKS

ISBN 0-373-76334-4

SLOW FEVER

Copyright © 2000 by Lois Kleinsasser

This edition published by arrangement with Harlequin Books S.A.

Visit Silhouette at www.eHarlequin.com

Printed in U.S.A.

Books by Cait London

CAIT LONDON

lives in the Missouri Ozarks but loves to travel the Northwest's gold rush/cattle drive trails every summer. She enjoys research trips, meeting people and going to Native American dances. Ms. London is an avid reader who loves to paint, play with computers and grow herbs (particularly scented geraniums right now). She's a national bestselling and award-winning author, and she has also written historical romances under another pseudonym. Three is her lucky number; she has three daughters, and the events in her life have always been in threes. "I love writing for Silhouette," Cait says. "One of the best perks about all this hard work is the thrilling reader response and the warm, snug sense that I have given readers an enjoyable, entertaining gift."

Dear Reader,

Happy Anniversary, Silhouette! It's been super fun, working with Silhouette's great editors, and sharing my stories with readers around the world. I'm a reader, too, and Silhouette stories are the best, ranging from humor to drama to action, from the dark and dangerous, hard and haunted heroes, to the lovable guy/friend next door, and from everyday women like myself, coping with life, to those women who have yet to meet their challenges. Just by opening a Silhouette book, I can visit places I've never been; I can be cool in the heat of summer by reading a story set in the mountains, or I can be drawn into a fast-paced romantic mystery. Then there's the well-done romance that always leaves readers happy. The span from sweet to sensual is a comfort zone for any woman; top executives are now carrying Silhouette books in their briefcases, just waiting for a break when they can step away and relax with good writing and a good romance. Whatever readers love, Silhouette serves it up with very special style.

As an author, I feel very special to be included in Silhouette's family, from my first book, *The Loving Season,* through the Tallchief miniseries, and all the books and families I'm currently creating. I hope for many more books and years with Silhouette. With new romantic stories pouring from the variety of authors and styles and Silhouette's special care, we'll be reading lots of good stuff for many anniversaries to come!

Cait London

The Women of Freedom Valley
Montana, 1882

Magda Claas   **Fleur Arnaud**   **Anatasia Duscha**   **Beatrice Avril**   **Jasmine Dupree**

Anna Claas m. Paul Bennett

Tanner Bennett

Kylie Bennett

Miranda Bennett

Cynthia Whitehall   China Belle Ruppurt   Fancy Benjamin   Margaret Gertraud   LaRue

To Mary Jo

Prologue

Town of Freedom 1882
From the journal of Magda Claas—

I have sisters, not of my blood, but of my heart. Women alone in a rough new land without protection, we formed a family. We settled in this valley bordered by high soaring mountains and traveled by men seeking wives. In this rough land, called Montana by the Indians, we'd come from all parts of the world. Some of us had thrown away hope, our lives ruled by men, yet it glimmered boldly when we decided to take this valley for our own and to call it "Freedom."

That is how I feel. These women, and more coming to the town we have created, are my sisters. We want to command our lives, to work hard and to be respected. We want love and husbands, too. We know now, after surviving a

*year in this beautiful valley, that we are strong and we
have pride in what we have built. Not one of us will easily
toss that away.*

*So we cherish each other as would a family, and we set
our conditions for the men who want us.*

*Love? Will it come to each of us? Is it too much to ask
of a woman's life? There are bargains to be made, but it
is the hope of every woman to find peace and love. Peace?
I am told that there is no peace around me, for I am too
busy with life.*

*With dreams and conditions, we, the women of Freedom
Valley, build our town. Let it be known through this rough
land that we protect our sisters, and that any man wishing
a bride must first come to us, her family. He must present
himself as a prospective candidate, the same as he would
come asking a father for a daughter's hand in marriage.*

*He must abide by our Rules of Bride Courting and meet
the terms of the Women's Council. We will have our due
as brides and wives and we will come together as sisters,
though marriage bonds have tied us to husbands.*

*Magda Claas
Town of Freedom, Freedom Valley
Montana Territory, July 1882*

One

My daughter, Kylie, is fourteen and has just threatened to kill young Michael Cusack, or at best, make his life unbearable. In a mood, she can make grown men shiver, but not Michael. Two years older and toughened by life, Michael is seeking curvier, more womanly fare. His father was heavy-handed and drunken, and Michael is not a boy, rather a scarred soul in a boy's body. I've fed him and done for him what his pride would allow. But Michael isn't the loving sort, trusting his heart to others, and he's having none of either of my girls. Because he respects me, he will not toy with my daughters, much to their annoyance. Miranda is merely nettled, but Kylie will never forgive that trespass.

—From the journal of Anna Bennett, descendant of Magda Claas and the mother of Kylie Bennett Patton.

"Mom?" Unanswered, Kylie's call echoed through the

white two-story house. The mid-September night wind
slashed autumn leaves against the windows, and memories
whispered around Kylie.

"Mom?" she called again, her heart tearing, for Anna
Bennett would not be answering her children's calls. She
lay by her husband's side in Freedom Valley's small cem-
etery; a semitruck at a foggy intersection had cut her life
short just eleven months ago. "You're here, I know you
are, Mom," Kylie murmured.

Kylie's brother, Tanner, was now off on his honeymoon,
remarried to his childhood sweetheart, Gwyneth. They
would return to their ranch near Anna Bennett's tidy, small
farm. In her mother's darkened house, Kylie stood by the
windows, scanning the small sleeping town of Freedom. Its
cluster of twinkling lights spread into Montana's night
stars. In the three days since Kylie had returned, she'd
learned that little had changed in Freedom Valley. The
Rules of Courting and the Women's Council still managed
to nettle the Bachelor Club, composed of single men
banded together for protection.

Kylie knew most of them; they were her brother Tanner's
lifetime friends. They were more like her brothers, since
she and her sister, Miranda, had tried to make use of their
frequent visits to Anna's house. Only one of the tall, swag-
gering devastating males could really upset her—Michael
Cusack. *Back then, she'd wanted to leap upon him and tear
him to pieces.*

Grown up and divorced now, Kylie didn't want to think
about Michael Cusack. Before her mother's funeral and her
brother's wedding, she hadn't seen Michael in years, pur-
posely missing him on her frequent visits to her mother's.
An older, very tough looking Michael had been at Anna's
funeral and Tanner's wedding. According to Leonard at the
gas station, Michael had been back for three years and was
running a small electric service company—while he tended

the mysterious women and children who came to stay with him. Kylie tensed, nicked by the slight annoyance she always experienced when Michael's name hovered around her. Through her early dating years, Michael had cut short her experimental escapades with fascinating men. One look at Michael's dark, ominous expression and the fascinating men seemed to shrivel away. He had the hard, blunt face of a fighter, the mysterious jade-green eyes of a poet, a mouth that could be line-thin and cruel or curved with laughter and warmth. That tall, lean body moved restlessly, like a wolf prowling, never relaxing, always ready to spring. His black rough-cut hair and thick, gleaming brows, those fascinating long lashes, could ruthlessly grasp a woman's heart. His brooding, lonely storm-tossed look made a woman want to hold him tight, to snag that wild hair in her fists and claim him.

Kylie sniffed lightly and shrugged, dismissing the dark and dangerous bane of her young life. He'd been a challenge then and nothing more. He'd tripped her fighting instincts long ago, but she was wiser now. Though Michael had dampened her experimental years, he and his women weren't Kylie's problems. Kylie scrubbed the tears from her face. "Mom, I'm in the pits right now, but don't worry. I will work things out. My brother is off on his honeymoon—sailing the seas with Gwyneth—and I'm tending your house and their ranch. A baby-sitter for everyone but my own kids—oh, I know. It's a dark and lonely night and I'm deep into a pity party. I'm stressed from dealing with my ex-husband, the breakup of the business, and I'm supposed to be sorting over the things in your house. I can't, no more than my brother could when he came back to Freedom Valley. Instead, Tanner started a custom-made wooden boat company and remarried his ex-wife. So here I am and I can't bear to separate your things any more than he could. It's only logical that your homeless daughter came home to roost.''

Kylie swallowed the tears tightening her throat. A widow raising three children without a complaint, Anna had always been there for her children—and now she wasn't. During those hard years, Anna had managed the small twenty-acre farm, selling butter, eggs and vegetables. She'd midwifed and birthed a good share of the babies in Freedom Valley. She'd washed and ironed for others, sold her herbal soaps and ointments, and most of all she'd loved and tended her children—and others who needed a kind heart. From her mother, Kylie had learned how a gentle, caring touch could heal. Kylie had learned the first elements of her profession as a massage therapist from Anna. ''So here we are, Mom. I'm back home again. Single white female, recently divorced, with a zero bank balance, and all I can do is polish your furniture.''

Kylie could almost hear her mother say, *You'll do fine. Make the best of it. Pick yourself up, dust yourself off and get on with life. Whatever is troubling you, deal with it as best you can,* her mother had said. *In the lonely hours, lemon and beeswax and plenty of good cherished furniture is a fine way to deal with troubles.*

''I failed at everything, Mom. My life, my dreams, my marriage. I came away with nothing but a few things packed into the back of my pickup.''

Mmm. And other people haven't failed? You came away with yourself and I'd say that is something. You're strong and you're good and you're talented. Take your time, deal with it and go on.

''I love you, Mom. I always will.''

Love yourself more, Kylie. You're a special person, giving light to dark, troubled souls. The world needs your laughter and energy and your beautiful, loving heart. You heal with your hands and your laughter.

"I did take in a few strays, didn't I?" The Bennett house had always overflowed with Kylie's refugees—even the box of newborn mice that she'd wanted to keep, and baby birds tossed to the earth by the winds.

You're strong, Kylie. You love to tend those who need you, but take time for yourself, too. Mend and go on.

"Is that what you did after Dad died? Kept us all fed on a threadbare budget, worked until you dropped, and still loved everyone around you, tending them?" Kylie had only been eight, but even then she'd known that she could never give her heart to a man who was less than her father— "Why did I have to marry Leon then?"

Her mother's soft reminder floated in the shadows. *Sometimes the helpless take advantage of a good heart, honey. Don't worry so—*

"Mom, I need you—" The shadows didn't answer this time, but the scent of Anna's herbs and her baking still clung to the house as Kylie wandered through it. The pantry was lined with Anna's canning jars, seeds and dried herbs neatly labeled, the clutter of hot water kettles and pressure cookers and juice makers ranged across one shelf. In a shallow basket, bars of lavender soap were neatly wrapped in plastic and tied with ribbon, waiting to be taken to Anna's customers.

In the shadowy room familiar to Kylie, the dim light gleamed upon a tall bottle labeled Blackberry Wine. The cork had been dipped in wax, and cording wound around the base, neatly finished in a bow and waiting to be tugged.

Kylie inhaled the scents flowing through her like memories. "Mom, I don't suppose you ever had a pity party, did you? Just to get everything out of your system, so you could go on?"

She could almost hear her mother's soft, knowing laughter—then Kylie remembered when she was nine and had awakened for water. Her father had been gone a year then.

Life had changed for the Bennett family and Anna hadn't complained about the hard work, the long nights mending and struggling to support her family. Yet all those years ago, in the kitchen, her mother's face had been covered with a mud pack and her hair was coated with mayonnaise. She had been soaking her work-worn hands in an aromatic soapy water, clear fingernail polish at the ready. A bottle of blackberry wine had been opened; Anna's glass was half full. Kylie had stared at her usually neat mother, and Anna had said, "There are times when life hits a woman hard, and it's best she pamper herself a bit, undergo a cleansing of sorts. And then she goes on. That's what I'm doing now—dealing with the woman in me. When it's your time, you'll know."

"It's my time tonight, Mom," Kylie said. "Thanks. I love you."

Whoever knocked persistently at the front door wasn't giving up and they were interrupting her blackberry "glow." Careless of the plastic wrap sheathing her naked body, Kylie jerked open the door. Through her mellow mood, the music of the tranquillity tape flowing around her, she saw the man she once detested. There was no mistaking the width of his shoulders, that hard, blunt face and untamed hair. She eyed him warily; she wasn't certain she didn't still hate Michael Cusack. Once, she would have hurried out the back door to let air out of his motorcycle tires. Once, she would have dumped water balloons on his head from the second story of her house. She would have written creative passages in bathrooms, like "Michael Cusack sucks eggs" or "Cusack has a fatal and contagious disease." Now she only wanted to be alone, sharing her blackberry wine with her mother's soothing presence. The blue clay facial mask cracked when she stated, "It's midnight, Michael. Go home to your harem."

In the light passing through the opened door, Michael Cusack loomed over her, even more rugged and dangerous looking than that night thirteen years ago when he'd plucked her from a mechanical bucking bull she'd been riding on a dare. "I could have ridden it, you know. Go away."

He rubbed his jaw, black eyebrows drawing together as he studied her. The scar ripping across his jaw was old and deepened his dangerous look. The September wind whipped at his shaggy black hair, his dark green eyes lighting with humor as he looked down at her. "I usually check on Anna's place as I pass. The yard pole light is out. What's with that getup and the goo on your face?"

"And I never liked being called 'short stuff.' Don't do it ever again. You did that at Tanner's wedding two weeks ago when Miss Bosom was draped around you." Kylie wanted to make certain he knew exactly his crimes of the past. She resented the inches up to Michael's six-foot-two height. At her eye level, the width of his chest was covered by a black sweatshirt. Well-worn jeans ran the long powerful distance between his black motorcycle boots, and Kylie launched her next volley without reservation. "It didn't bother me at all that you never asked me to ride on the back of your motorcycle."

"Okay," he said slowly in that gravelly voice that could raise the hair on her nape and his eyes hadn't moved from her plastic wrapped body. Humor softened the lines on his face. "You used to be a stick. Things have changed."

She jabbed him with her finger and carelessly tossed away the challenge that sprung from his narrowed green eyes. "Hey, buddy. I've been having a hard time, okay? Mom and I are having a little chat, and you aren't invited. I'm trying to lose weight fast, to feel better about myself, and I'd heard about this somewhere—whether it works or not, I don't know. But I'm activating, buddy. I'm not just letting myself wallow in things that weren't. When I'm up to speed, I'll get a good exercise program and drop the comfort foods.''

"Mmm. Too bad. The curves suit you," he murmured, his voice lowering a notch. His eyes roamed slowly up to her hair, propped high upon her head to escape the various mud packs and cleansing treatments she'd concocted. The tiny waves were exciting, not gracefully waved and tamed but wild and gleaming and soft as silk…just the kind a man wanted to spread his fingers into and feel drag against his body. Then his gaze dropped to lock onto her flattened breasts; her nipples peaked despite the transparent confinement and his mouth went dry.

Kylie swallowed tightly. She'd forgotten she'd opened the door wearing only the plastic wrap, to keep in the almond and herb oil mixture she'd concocted. The plastic wrap rattled slightly as she shivered, aware that Michael was slowly looking down the length of her body. She closed the door and turned off the living room light, tossing him a big "I want to be alone" hint.

Michael sucked in the night air and Kylie's scent and tried to drop his heart rate to a mere full-throttle race. Kylie's face had lost that round young look, her cheekbones slashing against the blue goo on her face. He mourned the shadows beneath her eyes and welcomed the blue burning slash of her eyes. As a child, she'd fascinated him. As a teenager, she'd made his blood churn. As a woman, she could devastate him. He recognized the hardening of his body and pushed away the thought of having her.

Anna Bennett's daughter wasn't for the likes of him. She'd be after a man's heart and he was lacking in that area; she deserved a family man, and he'd never wanted those ropes strangling him again.

Finding Michael Cusack on her mother's front porch wasn't exactly calming, a real dent in Kylie's healing ritual.

A massage therapist and schooled in anatomy, and as a woman, she knew after one look down Michael's tall body that he was in perfect physical shape. From the fit of his black leather jacket, she knew that his biceps, triceps, deltoids, and pectoral muscles would be powerful and bulky beneath her hands. Under his sweatshirt, his flat stomach probably rippled with muscles. She didn't want to think about the abductor muscles occupying his inner thighs, or the quadriceps of his thighs. Beneath his jeans' back pockets, his backside's gluteus maximus muscle would be firm and powerful. Over it all, his skin would be firm and warm and fine.

Before she closed the door her flush—around the area of the blue mask—amused him, for he recognized a woman's awareness of him. He also knew how well she could hate. Yet, it was fascinating to watch those blue eyes darken, prowling over his body, evaluating it as if he had potential to fulfill her needs. The sensual tug curled around him, though he knew Kylie would never see him as her heart mate.

She still hated Michael Cusack, she decided, as she peered out into her mother's driveway. His metallic gray Cusack Electric service truck was parked next to her white economy pickup; he wasn't going anywhere. Easing away the lacy curtain that shielded the front porch, Kylie saw Michael sitting on her mother's porch swing. It was the same porch swing upon which teenage Kylie had tried to vamp him. She'd wanted desperately to see if Michael Cusack's famed tongue could make steam come out of her ears. Not even the socks stuffed in her bra had added to her allure. Michael had laughed, the very worst offense to a potential first-time vamp.

Now the long, hard length of his body contrasted with the lace curtain framing him. Kylie held a sofa cushion up to her chest and rapped on the window. He turned to her

and when she waved him away, he shook his head and
grinned that fascinating beautiful grin as if he were a boy
again, a boy who had forever devastated her.

Kylie dropped the curtain, and grabbed another pillow to
cover her backside. She shuttled through the darkened
house as fast as her plastic wrapped legs would carry her.
She took another sip of her mother's blackberry wine and
shook her head. Michael wasn't going anywhere until she
disposed of him properly.

Minutes later, she jerked open the door again, quickly
tying a flannel robe around her plastic encased body. "People will see you sitting there and you know how the gossip
will spread."

He lifted an eyebrow and Kylie closed her eyes. "Okay.
Come in," she said with all the warmth of the doomed.

As she stood holding the door open for him to pass,
Michael looked even bigger than she remembered. Though
bulkier now, he was still lean and moved gracefully. He
carried with him dark tasty edges that she'd never know. He
wouldn't fit on her massage table. She'd have to use
the fold-out extensions— Her fingers flexed; she didn't
want to think of Michael's body beneath her hands…all
that lean, long body packed with cords and muscles and
wrapped in tanned skin. She wondered if the deep tan on
his face matched the shade on his—

Her fingers flexed again as he dipped his head to take a
quick kiss. Stunned, she watched him lick his lips, tasting
hers. Her hands ached to grab his hair, those thick shaggy
black strands, and to tether him for another kiss. She licked
her lips, tasting his and wondered what she had been thinking. His eyes were just as green as she remembered, framed
by dark lashes. Humor deepened the lines fanning from his
eyes and danced upon his lips as he drawled, "Blackberry
wine. You're tipsy, right?"

"You're interrupting my party," she said when she could struggle past the sizzling burn on her lips.

"I've been there," he said gently, easing his finger through the curls on top of her head. "Want to tell me about it?"

"No. Get lost." If she could have packaged that dark, brooding male scent, she could make a fortune. He smelled of the night and secret longings that most women couldn't refuse—but Kylie would.

"Can't leave. Told Tanner that I'd watch out for you while he and Gwyneth are on their month-long honeymoon."

"Big brothers. Who needs 'em?" Kylie muttered, uncaring that her tone reflected her dark and evil mood.

"What's the problem?" Michael asked, settling down on the sofa. He stretched his long legs out to the footstool that held her sea salt foot soak, peppermint foot cream, and bright red toenail polish. He placed his hands behind his head and studied her intently.

Kylie tossed away the uncomfortable, slightly guilty emotion that he had caught her in a criminal act. Anna had never allowed heavy drinking in her home. At the midnight hour and the changing of her life, she wasn't drunk, but a nice toasty "mellow." She was taking steps—the next major one was to do her toenails. She was actively dragging herself out of the post-divorce bog. She was jumping from a bad plateau in her life to her future.

She'd use him. Michael could always be trusted as a confidant. She lit the candles her mother had made, beeswax mixed with chamomile and ylang ylang. She'd shared that with her mother, the love of herbs and their uses and together they'd distilled the chamomile from her mother's herb garden. Kylie's plastic wrap rustled as she settled down beside him and indicated the spread of blackberry wine, cheese and crackers and rich, rich chocolate truffles which she had been slathering with her mother's raspberry jam. Michael poured wine into her glass, sipped and closed his eyes to enjoy. They were chums in this, the appreciation of Anna Bennett, a woman who had loved and tended them. "You'll have to do," Kylie said finally as she dipped the chocolate into the jar of raspberry jam.

She dipped a finger into the jam and suckled it thoughtfully as she studied Michael. "You seem tense. I suppose it's the reflex you got from back in the days when I was interested in you—when I was a child," Kylie said, sucking the rest from her fingertips. "I'd give you a massage, but right now I'm concentrating on my healing process and aligning my chakras. I'm in the ceremonial mode now—dispensing with the old to make a clean cut for the new me. I'm not usually self-indulgent, but I've got to deal with the pits before moving on. Meditating isn't cutting it."

His breath was rough and had a catching sound. His voice was deep and husky and uneven. "I'll take a rain check on the massage."

"You're not a massage kind of guy. Well, sports massage maybe. You have to give yourself over to relaxing to get the full impact, and you won't give a part of yourself away like that. You never have, not even when we were younger. You always seemed sort of coiled and ready to strike. I can't imagine you really unwound and relaxed," Kylie said, noting Michael's honed features, his clean-cut jaw and dark gleaming eyes. The candlelight drifted along his glossy lashes and softened the harsh lines across his forehead and beside his mouth. She leaned closer and scanned his face. At Tanner's wedding, the scar on Michael's jaw had shocked her. She hadn't asked how he'd gotten it, because Michael was a very private man. The chances of getting an answer were none to zero. "You could use some moisturizer. I was just getting ready to do my legs. I could shave you and—"

"No. I'm not into mutual-benefit preening." Michael's tone said he was just as immovable as when he'd tugged her off that bucking mechanical bull, plopped her over his shoulder and packed her out of the tavern to take her home.

Payback for the bucking bull incident and other matters would have to wait as Kylie dealt with her immediate healing process. She settled for needling him. "Mmm. Sun weathered skin. Tiny white lines at the corners of your eyes. You're only thirty-four, Michael. Your women will have you turned into an old man before your time. You'll have hair on your shoulders and be in the old men's turkey-neck club pretty soon. Moisturizers can help. I hope you're using a sunscreen."

He smiled slightly before Kylie stuffed a cheese topped cracker against his lips. There was just the slightest resistance before he accepted the companionable gift, and his lips opened. The heat from his mouth burned Kylie's fingertips as she drew away. A nervous little tingle shot through her as he studied her.

The trembling of her fingertips shot through him, surprising him. Other women had fed him, flirted with him, but Kylie wasn't on his list of potential bedmates.

"Okay, here's the scoop," she said, preparing to use Michael's ears to the fullest. He'd always been a good listener, despite his own rough life. Even then, he hadn't let too many people close to him, except Anna who thought of him as a son. "My mother would have adopted you," Kylie said softly, remembering how Anna cared for Michael.

He studied the strands flowing through his fingers, considering the light dancing upon them. "I know, but she had enough problems. I wasn't going to add to the mix. Keep on track. You're still running in all directions at once... I like the way your hair feels, the way it ripples against my hand."

"Now that *is* jumping tracks and not keeping to one direction." She'd tied her hair on top of her head with a blue ribbon, keeping it free of the various face masks. "I wasn't lucky enough to have Tanner's deep waves or Miranda's sleek, straight hair. Oh, no, I have this stuff, too curly if it's short. You could cut it for me, so short it couldn't curl. If it weren't so cold, I might try to shave it."

"No, thanks. I like long hair and the sky-blue color of this ribbon. It matches your eyes." Michael gently tugged the ribbon free and her hair spilled around her shoulders.

"I just haven't had time to deal with my hair or anything else—like a really good pedicure. It's been a busy year." Kylie settled deep into her thoughts, allowing Michael's toying with her hair to soothe her. "I thought when I got married, it would be forever."

"Did he hurt you?" Michael asked slowly, almost too carefully.

"He was a wimp. What can I say? Leon knew better. I'm in better shape than he was, faster and more flexible." Kylie pushed back the sleeve of her flannel robe to flex her muscle. The robe gaped, her breast leaped against the plastic and Michael sucked in his breath. She supposed this was because he was impressed with women who kept themselves in shape. She'd had to be physically active to stave off the emptiness of a sexless marriage. "But it didn't help my ego to work like a dog, try to build our business and then find him layered on my massage table with his girlfriend under him. The next thing I know, the company is belly-up, we're bankrupt and getting a divorce. He's married to Sharon now, a very good aerobics instructor. I sent a toaster, the wide-enough-for-a-bagel kind, but I really couldn't live with his suggestion—a communal sort of thing. I grew up here and though I married outside the permission of the Women's Council and The Rules for Courting, my values are still pretty much those of Freedom

Valley. You know me—I just jump into life. Well, this time my instincts—that I could make this marriage work—were dead wrong.''

Long ago she'd discovered the deep basic instinct she had for nurturing, sometimes unwisely. Leon had been a user, knowing how to push her need-to-help buttons. To be truthful, much of what had happened was her fault. She knew that she should have made him take more responsibility, but in a misguided sense of wifeliness, she'd taken most of the work load…and Leon, of course, was only too happy to give his share to her. "I can't place all the blame on Leon. By doing too much, I took away some of his feeling of accomplishment that his ego required. He's perfectly capable of running a spa. I just gave him too much time to play.''

Her head was a little heavy now, and Kylie rested it on Michael's shoulder. "I tried college, because it was important to Mom and Miranda and Tanner. After two years, I knew I wanted something else. I met Leon while working in a San Francisco health spa and retreat. I was studying for my license and met him at a Shiatsu conference…he's excellent at Shiatsu and reflexology, women used to praise his technique, though I never experienced it. Our interests were the same and I considered us to be Yin and Yang. Not an argument in our entire relationship. Leon never argued. He considered it beneath him. Now I'm thirty-two—was married for nine years, and worked so hard to build a business. I should have come home to see Mom more. Leon didn't want children and I agreed to wait—looking back, I don't think I would have wanted them to have his jaw. Leon had a really weak jaw and we hadn't had sex for years.''

Beneath her head, Michael's heartbeat seemed to have picked up pace. "I need sex, Michael. I'm a physical woman with needs. My clock is ticking and *she's pregnant with my baby!*''

''Your baby?'' Michael asked in that very wary tone as if he were picking his way through a field of land mines.

''Well, the baby that I eventually wanted. I wanted to be like Mom, to have a family and care for them, and to make her a grandmother. Leon wasn't up to par, and sex with him wasn't that good, and it's my only experience. Instinctively I knew his performance might lack as a baby-maker. I'm a nurturer, a loving woman, I need sex, and I've got nowhere to go with all my energy. It's frustrating.''

''Don't drink any more wine, Kylie,'' Michael said rather shakily after a long hesitation.

''I'm just mellow, not drunk. I never drink. It's the ring,'' she said, flopping back on the sofa to rest her head upon a pillow. Michael's shoulders were too hard for real relaxing.

''Ring?'' he repeated slowly, looking at the flannel robe that had just parted full-length to reveal her plastic coating.

''Ring! Wedding ring!'' Kylie waved her left hand and the gold band that had symbolized her marriage in front of him—because he didn't seem to be following her logic easily. His eyes slowly drifted from her body to her hand as Kylie said, ''I can't seem to just take it off. I mean what would I do with it? It's got to be a ceremony of sorts. A burial in a tin can, that sort of thing.''

''What's this mummy act?'' Michael asked, his fingertips smoothing the plastic on her thigh. They dug in slightly and his expression did that tight, darkening thing again. ''Take it off.''

The deep, raw edge to his order was unfamiliar. The dark, rich tone curled around Kylie, and she got that odd prickly feeling again. She studied Michael closely and pushed away the warning signals. Tonight, wrapped in plastic and dealing with the past, her logic could be akilter. She was having an off-night and not about to be intimidated by his order. "I have to take care of the man-catching equipment. Moisture is good for old divorced women who have to rebuild their lives. The prune look isn't appealing to potential sex-partners."

"You're thirty-two, Kylie, not ninety," Michael said roughly. "Take it off, dress in something else and I'll take you down to Valentina Lake where you can throw in the damn wedding ring and do what you have to do." Michael's voice was dark and rich, almost a growl. He scowled at her, poured another glass of wine and this time downed it quickly.

The idea appealed to Kylie, like the perfect maraschino cherry atop the nuts atop the banana split. She considered going to the lake, the drama of September winds sweeping across the lake as she hurled the ring into the dark mysterious depths. Michael was perfect for drama and late night adventure. "Good idea, but wrapping myself took a good hour. The stuff clings to itself and it will be a real job to take it off."

"I could help," Michael offered quietly, studying her with those dark forest-green eyes. Suddenly the air crackled with electricity, raising the hair on Kylie's nape as she scooted off the couch.

The tight binding around her knees almost caused her to fall back again, but Michael's broad palm flattened on her backside to push her upright. He had that closed-in, dark brooding look and the air seemed to steam around him as she wrapped her flannel robe around her protectively. "Mmm, no thanks. I'll be right down."

Two

Healing hands are a gift and so is a gentle, loving heart. If I could have my wish, there would be more people like my daughter, Kylie. When she is a woman, that kind, patient nature could be her undoing. Yet, there hovering cold in the shadows, the most lonely, torn heart will open to her healing touch.
—Anna Bennett's Journal

At two o'clock in the morning, Michael stood in the shadows of the pines bordering Valentina Lake. Outlined in the moonlight, Kylie stood with her ring clenched in her hand. She looked too small and alone, and he wanted to wrap her in his arms. He'd always wanted to protect Kylie, even when she was a girl and tormenting him.

She was all woman now—defenseless, explosive, steaming with sensuality. She moved like a dancer, and each succulent curve had called out to him. Michael frowned, unfamiliar with the hard desire riding him. The way her mouth had curved around the word "sex" had drained his mind and filled his loins. Holding her to comfort wouldn't work, not with his body hard and needing the warmth of hers. Michael lifted his face to the cold night air, scented with pines and Kylie's earthy womanly fragrance. He trusted the solitary life he'd built with Anna's help. He didn't trust himself with Kylie, not the hot raw need that had leaped to life when she'd opened that door. He turned up his collar against the cold wind sweeping down from the mountains and knew that Kylie's unpredictable and volatile moods could trigger emotions he couldn't afford. The hard jolt of seeing her almost nude had hit his body with the impact of a brand. He could do little but sink onto Anna's porch swing.

It was the same porch swing on which fourteen-year-old Kylie had tried to vamp him with Anna's flowers and herbs perfuming the summer air. Anna Bennett's daughter was off limits to a man who had little to offer. Michael accepted that he had no heart to give, no future to offer a woman. And yet tonight, he'd wanted to wrap his fists in that soft, wild storm of silky hair and devour her from head to toe.

She had him going again, he brooded darkly and resented his inability to deny the attraction. He'd known she was alone at the midnight hour and the need to see her was unnatural for a man who preferred his solitude. At Tanner's wedding two weeks ago, Kylie had been pale and taut, but she never let anyone see her shadows. Michael had wanted to hold her then, but one searing stab from Kylie's blue eyes told him she wasn't in a friendly mood.

Women should have digital readings across their foreheads that prepared a man for their emotions. Michael rolled his shoulder, aware of his tense muscles. With Kylie in his vicinity, anything could happen.

Insight into her failed marriage made Michael want to

punch something—preferably her ex-husband. A controlled martial arts expert, Michael leashed his dark mood. He didn't want attachments, not even with Kylie's soft heart. Was he with her now because of his tenderness for Anna?

Michael didn't trust the storm of emotions circling him. *He should have known better than to bring her here, with the night wind churning the past and mocking his fascination for her.*

Dressed in a short wool plaid jacket and tight jeans, Kylie stood with her back to him, her legs braced. "I can't do it, Michael," she said. "I wanted my marriage to last like Mom and Dad's. I thought I could make it work. I wanted— I know you've had women, but did you ever marry?"

Michael walked slowly to stand behind her; a strand of her hair floated on the wind, snagging gently upon the stubble on his cheek. He wrapped his finger around the silky softness and brought it to his nose, inhaling the fresh clean scent. This wasn't the Kylie who as a child had pestered him. This was Kylie, a woman trying to make sense of her life. He wouldn't touch her—she was too sweet and pure and...too damn voluptuous, looking like Mother Earth when she opened the door. Little had kept him from reaching out and placing his hands over her breasts, from devouring her mouth. He'd wanted to be in her, enveloped by her, holding her tight and— Michael breathed unsteadily, shaken by the deep primitive instincts to take Kylie, to bond with her.

He closed his eyes, remembering how many women he'd helped who had had men with those same unleashed instincts. He realized now that his hand was trembling, the hard impact of his need still circling him, but mixed with tenderness now. Michael's life hadn't prepared him for tenderness.

She looked at him over her shoulder, her eyes silvery

and haunted in the moonlight. "Help me. Talk to me. Tell me why dreams go so wrong."

He caught the windswept hair curling about him in his fist, tethering it gently and rested his hand upon her shoulder. He'd known her all her life and respected her family. He shouldn't be here with her, her soft body leaning slightly, trustingly back against his. The curved nudge of her bottom against him thrust a white-hot need into his lower body, startling him. His free hand shot to rest on her hip, his fingers latched to the rich curve. He was acting as her brother, he reminded himself, and he would not take advantage of Anna Bennett's daughter. He could see Anna in Kylie and Miranda, that loving nature. A man like himself—one too scarred by life—could easily tear Kylie apart. He forced his fingers to loosen and eased his hand away, shoving it into his pocket so as not to touch her. "I don't know about dreams."

As a child, his dreams had been torn away from him. He'd been ashamed of his life, but Anna Bennett had given him pride. Clean, patched clothes and a full stomach had done wonders for his self-esteem.

"Life is made of dreams, Michael. Everyone dreams. It's a part of life. Without dreams, nothing could happen— would happen." Kylie's eyes searched his face, reminding him of Anna's.

With Anna's help, he'd found a measure of peace in Freedom Valley. As the town's bad boy who could potentially infect other righteous men, he'd been labeled a "Cull" by the Women's Council. He wasn't expected to follow the traditions of the Founding Mothers, the women who had begun the traditions of men courting women. Kylie should have those traditions.

"I never married," he replied, skirting the issue at hand. He'd determined long ago never to marry, never to love, because love of any kind brought heartache. Yet he had to know about Kylie. "Did you love him?"

"Leon? I knew it wasn't exactly a steaming love-match. He has a great family, and I thought he'd have the same values as I. It's been months since the massage table discovery and my hurried divorce. I'm past the hurt stage, now I'm just mad at myself for wasting my life. Nine years…zip…gone, trashed. I was a virgin on my wedding night—I'm that old-fashioned." Kylie turned back to the dark lake and her fist pushed back at him. "Help me."

Virgin. Michael closed his eyes and tried not to think of Kylie's small soft body, another man loving her. He regretted drawing his hand from the confinement of his jeans pocket; he regretted the need to hold her tight and safe. "Are you ready? Maybe you'd better think about it."

"No. I want to do this now and get it over. Thinking won't change anything. I've got to get on with my life."

Michael breathed unsteadily and enfolded Kylie's small hand in his. "At the count of three, right?"

The gold circle spun an arc into the moonlight and then slid silently into Valentina Lake. Kylie was silent for a long time, and Michael prayed she wouldn't cry. Even as a child, when Kylie cried, a part of him went all weak and soft. "You'll be okay," he murmured finally, nettled that she was spending so much time grieving over a man who didn't deserve her.

He stepped back, determined not to hold her. He couldn't allow her softness to blur the truth of what he was, and he'd keep his distance.

Michael looked out to the whitecaps of the dark lake. It was rumored that a woman's soul walked the lake, restless to be reunited with her lover. He traced the waves and by habit, briskly pushed away romantic notions and the haunting legend. Kylie was right; he gave little of himself to others. But he knew how to protect women when the law was inadequate. The women he and Rosa Demitri rescued didn't deserve to be abused. They'd had their dreams torn apart by rough hands. Rosa had been his first rescue, and working with her ever since, he'd managed to change a few women's lives. He liked the feeling that he was passing on Anna's work, tending others. He brought the women and their children here to Freedom Valley where they could see how women should be respected and loved.

"'I'll be okay,' you say. What would you know about it? Besides the gossip says you've got a regular flow of women at your house and that you sport them all over town, never leaving them alone for a minute. It seems you've been the sperm donor for quite a few children. Boy, you must really have stamina."

"I like women," Michael returned slowly, amused at Kylie's nettled tone. *He loved holding the babies he'd delivered with Anna. Their mothers had needed Anna's healing hands and gentle midwifing. He loved holding the children close and snug against him, knowing that their new lives would be better.*

"How did you get that scar?" Kylie asked, touching the zagged white line on his jaw. Michael jerked his head away, fearing he would lean into her soft warm touch.

"Knife. Working as a bouncer in a bar has disadvantages... Did you have men customers? I mean, did you massage them?" He didn't want to think about Kylie's hands on other men, and that he should be affected by the thought rankled.

"Sure. For relaxation and sports injuries. I did lots of men... Mom said you went on to do high-priced security work."

"It paid the bills." His silent partnership in Newton Security Inc. still paid the bills for the women he sheltered. His needs were simple, but the regular dividends paid for new clothes. It also provided education so they could provide for themselves and a start in a new life. One of their early cases, Maureen Sanders, had sorted out her life and gone in for computer training, and she had recently sent Rosa a small ''payback'' check. Rosa's position as a substitute nurse for a national firm gave her insights into the case studies of abused women—information that she evaluated and forwarded to Michael. Not all women were candidates for rescue, but when protection and muscle was needed, Michael filled the job. He liked giving them a home in which to heal and not be afraid.

''How did you get from security work to electrical work?''

Michael skipped the electronics he'd set up for protecting clients—the alarms, sensors, cameras and listening devices. ''Just fell into it. Anna was my first. I rewired her house. Your dad did a good job, but some old wiring and the fuse box needed replacing. It took three weeks, and I enjoyed being with her.''

''Mom and Dad loved each other desperately. Her eyes lit up when she talked about him,'' Kylie murmured.

''She had soft, blue eyes like yours. Clear as the Montana sky, as if she knew the truth of life, free from shadows.'' Michael remembered Anna's love of her husband. Kylie deserved a man like that, solid, tender, loving. A man who could give her the traditions of Freedom Valley, and who would make a good father to the children she should have.

Michael didn't intend to have children—he could have inherited his father's dark side. His instincts told him to stay away from Kylie and settle for what he'd rediscovered in Freedom Valley. He'd watch another man hold her in his arms at the traditional Sweetheart Dance. He'd watch another court her and he'd be glad for her happiness, as Anna Bennett's daughter deserved. Michael inhaled the night air and Kylie's disturbing scent. Uncomfortable with his prowling, undefinable emotions, he said, "I'm hungry. I'll cook."

"Jerk. I'm dealing with a broken heart here and you're thinking of food."

"Let it go, Kylie. Move on." Michael's uncustomary impatience startled him. He didn't want to think of Kylie's love of life imprisoned by the past—too many women hadn't been able to move on, even with his and Rosa's help. Those women had eventually gone back to the men who had abused them.

"You think this is easy? Why are you here? Don't you have some woman's bed to warm?" Kylie asked, turning her frustration on him.

He studied her flashing eyes, now the color of moonlit steel and admired the sight. Kylie was a fighter and she'd struggle back to what she wanted, to the future she should have.

"I've done my share. I'm here because Anna was special. So are you." He would rather have that than her tears, mourning a man who had hurt her. Michael eased a wind-tossed ringlet away from her face, his thumb caressing the fine warm skin of her cheek. It had been five years since he'd last had a woman, and he had the unshakable feeling that last time he'd been doing the mechanics. That hard cold stark realization was enough to make him recheck his life and his values. He'd been shocked to discover that he'd become old-fashioned and that lovemaking should mean more than bodies locking to feed a hunger.

Maybe a little of Freedom Valley's old-fashioned ideas about love and romance had washed off on him in the three years since he'd been back. He studied Kylie's face, and knew that she deserved the best, the courting and the treasuring of a bride. He shrugged and moved away, shoving the lingering warmth on his hand into his pocket. Kylie's soft heart wasn't for the likes of him.

"If you tell anyone about tonight and how I'm feeling, I'll kill you," Kylie promised adamantly, glaring up at him.

"That might cost," he returned slowly, and enjoyed her flash of anger.

She punched him lightly in the chest and Michael caught her hand in his. It was small and delicate and yet strong. The impulse to bring it to his lips surged through him as their joined hands rested over his heart. He pasted a leer upon his face, just to remind her that he wasn't a tender man. Kylie ripped her fist away, rubbing it with her other hand. "I made your life miserable when you were chasing every girl in the countryside and I can do it again."

"I promise never to make fun of your concoctions for removing freckles again. They're rather sexy." Michael couldn't resist bringing her small fist up to his lips and kissing it. Kylie's stunned expression was worth the punch to his stomach that followed. "So how do you like your eggs cooked?" he asked, as she walked toward his truck and he reluctantly admired the sway of her hips in the moonlight.

She turned to him suddenly, looking very alone in the moonlight, her hair flowing around her. "I embroidered the pillowcases and tea towels for my hope chest. Mom wanted that. She wanted me to have all the values that she had, stuffing that chest for the home I'd have with my husband someday. I skipped all that, leaped right out there and hurt her. She was at our Justice of the Peace wedding in Kansas City, but I knew that she wanted me to be wearing white and coming down the aisle of Freedom's church. My hope chest is still in Mom's house and I can't bear to open it. Miranda left hers, too."

"Take it easy on yourself, Kylie. Anna loved you."

"She loved you, too. Don't try to deny that you loved her, either."

Michael thought of the woman he'd adored, the closest

thing to a mother that he'd had while growing up. "Yes, I did love her. And that is why I'm taking you home now. She wouldn't want you out here catching cold."

At four o'clock in the morning, Michael swung up on his horse, Jack. The gelding stomped and tossed his head, sensing Michael's restless mood. Michael sat on Jack for a time, studying the home he'd rebuilt for security, to protect the women he championed. A simple ranch house design, it was his first real home. Anna had helped him design the privacy elements, a woman's bathroom, a playroom and nursery for children that could be turned into a birthing room. A kindhearted doctor in a neighboring county would take care of the women when needed, managing birth certificate legalities. Thomas White quietly supported Anna's midwifing and both had tutored Michael to care for the women.

He hated the sound of women crying. The sounds were the first in his memory, his mother sobbing.

The night wind slid through the autumn leaves, rattling them in the starry night. In Anna's house, Kylie could be crying. She was just as sweet and prickly to him as ever, and now she was in pieces.

A sharp order to Jack sent him racing across the field. Another order and Jack sailed over a small fence, racing into the wide Montana countryside. Bent low on the gelding's back, Michael wanted to work off his dark mood before meeting Rosa two states away. Another restraining order hadn't worked and Mary Ann Lucas was pregnant and needed help. Michael didn't want his dark mood to complicate the discussion with Mary Ann's brutal husband. He didn't want mistakes that could ruin Mary Ann's chances for a new life. With Rosa, Michael dealt with details, efficiently blocking the women's past from their future.

Years ago someone like Mary Ann's husband had taken Michael's older sister's life, but there had been no one to protect Lily, not even the law. He'd made a vow upon discovering Lily's senseless violent death, that he'd protect other women like her. With each woman he rescued, he felt he gave back a little of what no one had done for Lily.

"Everyone knows that Michael Cusack is a Cull and that his service truck was parked outside your place for most of the night," Karolina Jones stated firmly the next day in her small, tidy community library. She slammed the Date Due stamp down on a library card and filed it neatly. An anonymous donor had just supplied the library with a hefty contribution that couldn't be traced. "If he weren't a Cull, but a man with a good reputation hunting a wife, you'd be called up before the Women's Council. He'd be obliged to go before them and ask to court you. They'd slap a Rules of Bride Courting handbook in his hands so fast, he wouldn't have time to run."

"'Fast Hands Michael' didn't get that reputation for nothing. He's been labeled a Cull by the Women's Council since he was thirteen, already hot to trot. Every girl rode on the back of his motorcycle—except me, of course, and Miranda and yourself."

Kylie smiled as she thought of her sister. Miranda had been elegantly nettled by Michael and his lack of interest in her as she was trying out her flirting skills. Sadie McGinnis, a member of the Women's Council, had already called as Kylie was struggling out of bed—reminding her that Michael's reputation was dark and that with the number of children visiting his house, he had the ability to impregnate the state of New York.

However, Michael had stopped to fix Sadie's front door light this morning and had informed her that the yard light at Anna's was more of a problem than he'd suspected. And, Sadie knew that though divorcées sometimes leaped into the arms of waiting male predators, Kylie—as Anna's daughter—was far too sensible. The Women's Council had decided to dismiss the incident. However Michael's Cull status remained. "Scandalous, just scandalous how many women he has visiting him in that house. No telling what goes on there. There are probably leopard skin throws and black satin on round beds in every room, push buttons to close the curtains and turn on seductive music. And the way they look at him, as if he were all they had in the world, their guardian," Sadie had said.

Kylie didn't want to think about Michael, or the way his dark study of her had sent off clanging warning signals. "Mmm. I don't want to talk about Michael. Are you still hunting information about LaRue and about the woman in Valentina Lake?"

"LaRue's the only one on the 1880s Founding Mother's Council who isn't really portrayed well. The woman haunting Valentina Lake is supposed to be nothing more than a legend. But once I find the right document, I'll verify that legend. They haven't named me 'Super Snoop' for nothing. I like mysteries and one of them is finding the person who is donating so much to the town. He paid the well digging company to go out to old Mr. Franks's farm and drill a new well. Several other incidents have happened, like the Williams girl, Netta, received a notice from an orthodontist that she should set up an appointment for badly needed braces. The Freedmans couldn't pay their medical bills and their mortgage was up—suddenly the bills were cleared. Weird things—but good things—are happening, and someone with money is behind them."

Kylie frowned, remembering the different packages her mother had found on their doorsteps. A widow on a tight budget and raising her three children, Anna had smiled softly when the packages revealed material and lace she couldn't afford. There were other modest gifts—earrings Miranda had wanted for a prom, a graduation watch for

Tanner and a golden locket and necklace for Kylie's six-
teenth birthday. A night shadow went slipping through her
mind—the image had haunted her since childhood, of that
shadow leaving the gifts on their back steps where they
could be easily found. While Karolina may have forgotten
her sleuth work from back then, pinpointing Michael's pur-
chases, Kylie hadn't. "He's still around then—the anonymous guy, the benefactor."

"None of my leads have paid off," Karolina said. "But
I'll nail him…. You know that all the single men are
worked up since you came home. Some of the married
ones, too. They're wondering what you'll do…. By the
way, Michael left town this morning, all dressed in black
and looking tough. He's going after another one of his
women friends—that's his *modus operandi*, that's the scenario. He leaves town for a few days and comes back with
a woman. He sure orders a lot of things after they arrive.
He just backs his rig up to the back of the post office and
piles in the boxes. Sometimes it's baby stuff. I know because I made it a point to 'accidentally' stop by and help
him load boxes. The labels are from women's catalog
stores—so what are your plans?" Karolina asked in one of
her typical fast-lane mind changes.

Kylie grinned at her friend. They'd known each other as
children, and Karolina was always packed with surprises.
"I'm all through the mad and crying part. Now it's time
for the reconfiguring, arranging my life and getting an income of some kind. I can't live at Mom's forever…."

"Why not? Anna would have liked you there, taking care
of her things. You have Anna's way of reaching people, of
making them feel good and alive."

Kylie nodded slowly. "I like helping people, making
them feel better. I learned a lot with Mom and then took
courses later. Some people are in the massage business to
make money, and they don't have a real feel for it. This is

the place for what I want to do, here in Freedom Valley. Come over for dinner tonight. I'm aching to get my hands into that tense neck of yours. We'll watch a movie and catch up.''

Karolina frowned and rubbed her neck beneath her prim lace collar. "It is tight. See? We need you in Freedom."

Two days later, Karolina squinted out to the road in front of Anna's house. She'd heard a car honk and another one return the sound, a greeting along lonely roads. Despite Kylie's relaxing massage, Karolina couldn't resist popping up and running to the window. She wrapped the sheet she had been lying on around her shoulders. "Quick. Get my glasses and don't get that massage oil on them, either."

"You're getting all tense again. Come back and let me finish massaging you. You really need the last relaxing part," Kylie said, handing Karolina her glasses.

"Pond scum. Womanizer. Cull," Karolina muttered as she scooted her glasses onto her nose. "That's Michael out there and he's got another woman with him. The moon is bright tonight and I see two heads. See? That is exactly why the Women's Council doesn't want him around good marriage candidates. He can't stick to one woman. Never has, so far as I know. He's following his typical M.O. He'll take her to his house. Then tomorrow morning all these packages will arrive. Let's go see what he's brought home this time."

Kylie watched Karolina scurry out of the room, draped in the sheet. "Spy on Michael? I don't think so. There are just some things that I don't care to know."

"I'm changing into my clothes—all black spy-stuff," Karolina called. "I'm going whether or not you are."

Kylie shook her head even as she jerked on her jacket. "We're not kids anymore, you know. I got into enough trouble with you back then."

Twenty minutes later, Karolina led down a backwoods path from the road to the knoll overlooking Michael's redwood and brick home. She parted the brush to view his yard, and in the dying light, Michael was holding the crying woman tight against him. Karolina tugged Kylie to crouch beside her, shielded by the brush.

In the moonlight, the woman's skin contrasted with Michael's sun-weathered skin and Kylie frowned, fighting the slight rise of jealousy. She'd wanted to huddle against Michael just like that. "Any woman with half a brain would know better."

"Huh?" Karolina removed her glasses to clean them with the edge of her cotton sweatshirt. "You got oil on my glasses, but my neck feels a lot better. You ought to set up shop here in Freedom. You can post an ad on the library bulletin board."

Kylie wanted to pit herself against something—someone—and forget about Michael's tenderness with the woman, the way he handled her gently into the house. "What was that you said about dancing down at the Silver Dollar Tavern?"

"My brother, Dakota, and the Bachelor Club usually show up there after a good-old-boy game of touch football. It's a good place to catch up on gossip, see if anything is happening that I might need to follow up."

"I haven't danced for a hundred years. Or played touch football. Let's go."

Karolina shook her head and studied Kylie's red sweater, jeans and boots. "I don't know if I'm up to that much excitement. You get those guys stirred up and no telling what will happen. You're not a stick anymore, you know."

"Don't you dare say a word about the weight I've put on, Karo." Kylie grinned at her lifelong friend. Thoughts of Michael and his women weren't ruining her recovery-from-divorce. She gave herself to the joy of running through the night with Karolina huffing behind her.

Three

Men may scorn a tender heart and a soothing hand but they need them just the same. I wish Kylie would stop stuffing socks in her underwear to give her curves. Her father used to say that he pitied Kylie's true love, for the man would have to be steady as a rock and fast to move, to keep firm hold of her.
—Anna Bennett's Journal

Four weeks later, at midnight in mid-October, Michael slowed his four-wheeler as he passed Anna's darkened house. Kylie's small economy truck wasn't sitting in its usual place beneath the big tree near Anna's driveway. Since Kylie had been back and Mary Ann had been staying with him, Kylie had been stirring up all the males in Freedom Valley. Michael didn't like wondering about Kylie's whereabouts or companions.

He knew she had seen him with Mary Ann, buying gro-

ceries for the undernourished woman. Kylie's blue eyes had
focused immediately on Mary Ann's slightly bulging
tummy and her accusing glare had burned Michael. She'd
stiffened, turned up her nose and had hurried down the
grocery aisle away from him. He'd heard that she was fast
and agile at touch football, and when she danced, she sizzled with so much sensuality that men stepped back to ad-
mire the flowing fit of her jeans and her sweater. With a
sense of humor and a ready laugh and compassion, Kylie
was on the dating block, and the unmarried men were circling her. Noah Douglas, John Lachlan, York Meadows and
the rest were salivating, getting worked up to ask Kylie for
a real date. They'd take their time, making certain they
wouldn't have to handle a woman on a divorcée's crying
jag, and then they'd move in.

Michael didn't like the tense lock of his body when he
thought about another man holding Kylie as they danced.
He didn't trust his need to hold her close and safe against
him. Just returned to Freedom Valley, Michael had helped
transfer Mary Ann's few possessions into Thomas White's
large home three hundred miles away. With a background
in nursing, Mary Ann would assume duties in Thomas's
doctor's offices, located in the house, and Thomas could
easily look after her tenuous pregnancy.

Tanner and Gwyneth had returned from their honeymoon. Just a field away from Anna's, their remodeled home
was also dark, but Tanner's and Gwyneth's trucks were
parked side by side, just as they would lead their lives.

Michael's hands clenched on his steering wheel as a deer
leaped across the country road in front of him. After a
month of dealing with Mary Ann's health and helping her
forge a new life, Michael's nights were sleepless and
haunted by the vision of Kylie's plastic wrapped, curved
body. He could still taste her kiss—could still remember

her scent, like violets, the rich earthy scent of meadows in sultry sunshine, and a disturbing, more sensual, feminine scent.

Kylie was an irritant in the life he wanted to move smoothly, without ties. He couldn't forget her and he wanted her, an unfamiliar emotion for a man who had trained himself to desire little else but money.

His vehicle's tires slid smoothly over the gleaming cobblestones of Freedom's town square, the 1880s two-story buildings lining it. Long ago, drovers passed through this town, celebrating after delivering their Texas cattle to Montana ranchers. Whatever woman-hunting ideas they'd brewed with their liquor were soon doused by Freedom's Women's Council. Men behaved like proper suitors in Freedom and some remained as good husbands. Others, who might have shared Michael's distaste for boundaries and rules and ties of the heart, were told to move on.

Store windows gleamed in the streetlights as he passed. The worn-smooth cobblestone road that led to the church was one he would never travel in the customary way of a bridegroom, nor was he likely to take his love before the Women's Council in an old-fashioned surrey. To court a woman of Freedom Valley by custom meant explaining why he wanted her in his life—as his bride and his wife— in front of a tough Women's Council. Michael couldn't see himself performing to their demands.

Kylie's small pickup was parked in front of the Silver Dollar Tavern. The thought that she'd be wrapped in another man's arms hit Michael like a Mack truck. The dark sweep of anger nettled. He parked directly behind her and damned himself for wanting to see her. The slamming of his door marked an intense emotion that startled him. Michael stopped on the sidewalk, listened to the jukebox music throbbing from the Silver Dollar and sucked in the crisp, calming night air. He didn't need excuses to go inside—he told himself he needed a break after a hard day. Stopping for a beer had nothing to do with his need to see Kylie. Inside the tavern, the slow music was loud and the floor was packed with dancers, bodies laminated together as they swayed.

One quick scan of the room and Michael found Kylie massaging Brody Thor's back as he sat leaning over the table, head resting on it, his arms dangling loosely at his sides. Dressed in a red sweatshirt and grass-stained jeans, Kylie was standing behind Brody, the owner and only employee of a concrete business. York Meadows, Koby Austin, his brothers—Adam and Laird—sat sprawled at a cluttered table. Their stares led to Fletcher Rowley, Gabriel Deerhorn, and Dylan Spotted Horse and Karolina's table. From the noticeable grass and mud stains on their clothing, they'd been playing touch football again.

Michael felt like touching something and it wasn't a football; it was Kylie. He recognized the men's contemplative, closed expressions, as they studied Kylie's curved body, flowing with the kneading movements. A sensual symphony of curls, Kylie's hair was propped upon her head. The drift of the tendrils along her delicate nape begged for a man's hand to ease them aside for a kiss on the soft curve.

After the first surprising wave of tenderness, desire slammed into Michael, stunning him, as he worked his path through the dancers. Lora Simmons pressed against him, running her hand over his chest. "Dance, handsome?"

"No, thanks." Michael moved away from Lora's perfumed curves and low-cut, tight sweater. He moved toward Kylie's grass-stained sweatshirt and jeans. He had the unshakable sense that the image of Kylie's plastic wrapped body had ruined him for other women. He tensed as he heard Brody groan in relief, Kylie's slender fingers digging into the areas along his spine. Brody's groans were too close to another sound that Michael didn't want men making under Kylie's touch.

She'd been honest in her need for sex that night at Anna's. Michael inhaled slowly and considered Kylie's expression, one of concentration on her task, her spiraling curls bobbing gently as she worked. She was healthy and strong and earthy. It wasn't his business if Kylie wanted to make love—or was it?

He stood beside Kylie as she worked on Brody, finding his scalp through his hair and massaging it. Michael looked slowly to the other men, one at a time, and knew that every one wanted to be the body beneath Kylie's strong, knowledgeable fingers. He knew his friends well enough to know that they'd deliberately strain a few muscles just to replace Brody's aching ones under Kylie's hands. "No," he murmured quietly and recognized the momentary challenging flash in the men's eyes.

Just noticing Michael, Kylie straightened and her expression immediately changed from one of concentration to one of frost. "Did *she* let you loose tonight?" she asked in a tone that could have frozen a forest fire.

"Dance?" he countered, dismissing her question and challenging her at the same time. Michael realized then that he'd wrapped his hand around her slender wrist, holding her.

He'd promised himself long ago that he wouldn't need anyone. And now he needed Kylie. He studied his scarred and darkly tanned fingers against her fairer skin, shocked by the knowledge that he'd wanted to claim her for his own. He slowly released her wrist and removed his black leather jacket, tossing it to Gabriel Deerhorn.

The night he'd seen her in another tavern, a nineteen-year-old girl on a dare, determined to ride that mechanical bucking bull, he'd burned with the same dark anger. It was the only mechanical bucking bull in the countryside—miles from Freedom Valley—and Kylie and her friends had dressed older, just to get into the tavern. She'd rocked upon the bull, testing herself, swaying with the movements too slow to be dangerous. She'd concentrated on her task, her body flowing sensually as she moved around and stood and sat and tested her skill. The rhythmic symphony of curves had men drooling and had sucked away Michael's breath when he'd first seen her. When he'd managed to pull his tongue off the floor, he told would-be takers that she was his wife and the baby needed her at home. Then he'd hauled her off that bull and she'd sulked at the lecture as he delivered her and her underage girlfriends each to their doorstep. The last one to reach her home, Kylie had simmered and then lunged at him. "Little girl," he'd said, trying to distance his need to give her a taste of what she'd been asking from him. "Take it inside and don't worry your mother."

It was just the same now; Michael couldn't breathe, couldn't move. *Kylie had always been his.*

The thought zinged through Michael, shocking him as Kylie's blue eyes darkened. His gaze slid to her lips and then slowly down her body, marking the sudden rise and fall of her breasts. "I asked you to dance. Yes or no?"

Kylie's chin lifted and she spoke quietly, only to him. The color of her blue eyes had changed to steel flashing up at him. "Tell me first—do you have that woman living with you now or not? And is it your baby?"

"Interested in me?" he asked, challenging her as he took her hand, laced her fingers with his and led her the few steps to the dance floor.

"I'm older and I'm wiser. I don't want to sit on the back

of your motorcycle now. And you weren't invited here, and just how much of my life did you tell your girlfriend?''

''Put your hands on me like you did on Brody and you'll find out more than you want to know,'' he murmured. His hand sought the curved indentation of her waist and hip to draw her close. For just an instant, his fingers dug in slightly to the soft curve, claiming her.

Michael breathed unevenly, stunned by his first experience to make certain this woman was his.

''Brody's back injury needs a good stroking treatment to relax—I'm not explaining anything to you.''

''"Stroking?"'' Michael repeated her term darkly, unfamiliar with the emotions storming him. The word brought the image of lovemaking slapping at him.

''Soothing him. It's a technique in Swedish massage.'' Her breath caught as his arm slid around her, holding her close against him.

She recognized that whipcord strength, moving too quickly for her to resist. He'd acted like that at the infamous bucking bull incident. His thigh pressed between hers, leading into a dance step, and Kylie tensed, moving stiffly to his direction. ''The Women's Council should have changed the rules that men always lead in dancing, too.''

''Good luck with that one,'' Michael murmured against her temple. He paused in a turn, and the movement took her off balance, leaning against him. He held her there to prove his point, that he could easily control her body, while there was little chance of her supporting his larger one. ''There are just some things a man does better. That irks you, doesn't it? Here, you lead.''

He stood still in her arms, waiting, and when Kylie pushed against him, he remained rock-solid. A smile lurked at his beautiful mouth as he tugged her against him again.

Michael rested his cheek against the soft froth of her hair, inhaling her scent as they danced. He'd never answered questions before, but Kylie was important to him. He gave her what he could: "It's not my baby. But Mary Ann needed me."

Kylie sniffed in elegant disdain, her body tense against his. "Mr. Good Guy. Or are you her ex-lover?"

He smiled at that slight nick of jealousy, and the aloof angle of her chin, proof that he didn't fall in the "I just don't care" zone. Kylie's emotions toward him had always run to the hot and hotter side. "She's a friend. Most women trust me."

"They shouldn't." Kylie leaned back to look up at him, her eyes searching his expression. "I don't know what my mother saw in you. No wonder you're a Cull. If the married men or the single ones associate too much with you, they'll be paying a high price with their wives and the women in their family. That's how it is here in Freedom Valley—a male Cull could contaminate a whole good barrel. I wouldn't be dancing with you now, but you're not above telling everyone about my—"

"Blackberry wine party? The plastic wrap?" As her eyes darkened and her mouth tightened, he waited for her to sulk.

"Worse. I'm afraid you'll say something about my need for—"

"Sex? No. I don't remember anything about your mentioning sex." *The hell he didn't; it only kept him sleepless and in a permanently hardened condition after dreaming of her soft body against his.* Her needs weren't for discussion, images of her curved body tossed dark and sweet upon his mind. Then Michael bent his head and kissed her slowly, thoroughly tasting all the dark, earthy, exciting nuances that were Kylie. "Ready to go home?" he asked against her hot cheek and tried to keep his body from hardening as she quivered within his arms.

"Not with you," she said firmly, warily, with lips that he now knew were soft and tender and evidence of a very warm, responsive woman.

That annoying wisp of tenderness curled through him, followed by the dark knowledge that every single male in Freedom Valley couldn't wait to court Kylie. Added to her curvaceous, fit and admittedly sensually deprived body, she was perfect wife material—sweet, caring, a natural homemaker and a loyal, supportive friend, and she'd want a home and a family.

Wife. The word echoed coldly around him. With his family's dysfunctional background, Michael wasn't made for the matching role of the homey picture—the husband, the father. Kylie deserved the whole picture and a man who knew how to fill his role.

"Okay." He nodded and released her. He ran his fingertip down her hot cheek and cherished the slight quiver of her lips as he stared at them. He took one last taste of those softly parted lips and caught her startled sigh into his mouth. Just there was her immediate warm response surging and hungry. He held the kiss a bit longer to convince himself the taste of hunger ruled her, too, just as it thundered through his blood.

Then he stepped back, signaled for his jacket and caught it when thrown to him. He walked out of the tavern as if Kylie's kiss weren't burning his lips. He forced himself to drive home, but once in the driveway, he sat quietly, stunned by the need to court and cherish Kylie and make her his bride. He'd never been a dreamer, wishing for things he couldn't have, and Kylie wasn't on his life goals list— a measure of peace was, living alone, helping the women who needed him. Anna had always said his time would

come, but Michael never suspected it would be Kylie, or
that his desperate need for a woman would become a reality.

Kylie needed time to deal with the aftereffects of her
divorce. She needed a good solid man like her brother and
the other men in Freedom Valley, who cherished and
courted their brides. Michael knew little about what ran
between a man and a woman, how to keep it safe and warm
and glowing. But he'd seen it with Paul and Anna Bennett,
and Kylie deserved the same care in a relationship.

Michael rubbed his hand along his jaw and the scraping
sound reminded him of how he must have looked to her—
tough, tired and wanting to lift her up in his arms and carry
her out into the night.

A throbbing headache lurked at his temples. He wasn't
the man for Kylie Bennett Patton, all-American sweetheart,
a woman meant for traditional courtship. In Freedom
Valley, according to custom, that meant that she'd be doing
the courting and pacing the relationship. She'd be asking
for dates and the trial marriage in which they lived together
and the Committee for the Welfare of Brides would visit
the home and—Michael heard his groan echo as he entered
his empty, shadowed house. He checked the security locks,
punched the message machine button and listened to Karolina's furious recorded threat. "Don't you think you can
jump my friend, Fast Hands Cusack. She's not going to be
one of your women."

"Thank you, Karolina. As if I needed that reminder."
Michael smiled slowly when the messages continued. His
stock broker had heard of a good investment and Mrs. Mor-
ley had decided her breaker box wasn't working. Mrs. Mor-
ley was lonely and loved company and Michael always
obliged her calls, though there was no electrical problem.

Whatever Karolina's opinion of him, he'd always liked

her. He infuriated Karolina on another level—her "Super
Snoop" powers couldn't delve into a life he wanted to re-
main very private.

He'd always preferred privacy, using it as a shield. In
contrast, Kylie was a whirlwind, diving into life, loving it.

He could taste more on Kylie's lips than sensual need—
he could taste a future that wasn't meant for him, and that
knowledge terrified him...because he could hurt her.

The next night, Kylie lay fully dressed on top of her
sleeping bag, studying the flames of her campfire. A fast
set of push-ups and sit-ups and running in place had left
her tired, damp with sweat, and still brooding about Michael's very knowledgeable kiss. Its tempting heat hovered
around her now. She could still taste the hunger on his
lips—too dark and stormy and mysterious. He'd lightly circled her lips with his parted ones and the exquisite torture
frustrated and heated.

After Michael's kiss, her personal thermostat was simmering; she'd needed the chilly mountain night alone with
her thoughts. With a supreme effort, she dragged off the
sweat-dampened bandanna from her forehead. Kylie listened to the slowing beating of her heart—it had raced
when Michael had kissed her and the sensual tug right there
on the dance floor had shot directly low in her belly. The
physical need to have him, to stop the aching, was overpowering—she wasn't certain what would have happened
if he hadn't walked away.

*She damned him for walking away as if he hadn't been
simmering, too.*

The small clearing was where her family had camped
every year, a stream tumbling nearby. After Michael's sizzling kiss, she needed time alone, away from the haunting,
tender memories of her mother. She wasn't certain that

Anna would approve of her fantasies—how Michael's powerful back would feel beneath her fingertips, how he would feel over her, in her and hungry.

Kylie moved her hand from her racing heart—its tempo wasn't only from her workout, but from the memory of how Michael had looked at her, as if nothing else mattered. With an effort, she sat up, pushed up her red sweatshirt and shimmied out of her elastic exercise bra. The firm tug required to slide it over her hips reminded her of the extra pounds she'd put on while lamenting her life. More comfortable now, she flopped the undergarment over her backpack and lay back onto her bedroll. Last night, her basic instincts had told her to run him down and have him.

Kylie ran her hands through her hair, lifting the sweaty ringlets away from her face onto her favorite pillow. Michael was a great big smudge on her peace of mind, but then he'd always been.

An autumn leaf swirled lazily down into the fire and ignited, just as she had when Michael's big hand had cupped the back of her head, positioning her for his kiss. An experienced man, he'd known how to hold her firmly in place, taking what he wanted. For an instant, the primitive image of a stallion overtaking a mare in season ripped through her. But even before that, Michael's mouth seduced; she'd been unprepared for the darker elemental storm that had followed—the seduction.

"Exactly what do I know about being seduced? Or seducing? Leon wasn't exactly hungry for me," she asked the moon above the pine branches. *But Michael was hungry, the tip of his tongue prowling her lips, gently invading her mouth to set off the rocketing heat within her.*

Kylie lay on her back, looking up at the clear Montana night through the stark, leafless branches of the aspens.

Suddenly a noise sounded too close and a tall, hard-looking man stepped into the firelight—"Michael!"

Dressed in a flannel lined denim jacket and jeans, he slung his sleeping bag and backpack from his shoulder to the earth. He suddenly crouched to place a hand on her chest, pinning her firmly to her sleeping bag. She caught his scent, that slightly spicy blend of aftershave and the dark nuances of his temper. "Your brother is worried about you. Notes like 'I'm going camping. Back soon,' don't cut it."

He caught her swatting hands easily, holding them in one hand as his other tested the damp strands around her face. His gaze ran down her sweat clothing, the damp vee at her chest, locking on the rapid rise and fall of her breasts. Suddenly Michael freed her hands as if they'd just scorched him and stood scowling down at her. He looked hard, the firelight deepening the lines bracketing his mouth and between his black slashing brows. "Let me guess. You're burning off excess sexual energy."

"I'm burning off pounds, not sexual energy," she lied, glaring up at him.

"Sure," he said flatly. "You had to come up here, alone, to do that?"

Unpredictable as always, she'd scared the hell out of him. This time of year, an early snowfall could take bears and wolves searching for food. She could have slipped, falling into those jutting, deadly ravines. He hadn't realized his blood could run so cold, or his fear could rise so high. He'd pushed himself up the mountain, half running, his sides aching, his heart pounding with fear, only to find her dreaming by her campfire, snug and warm. She had the ability to terrorize him and that frightened him, too. He didn't like the quivering emotions within him, the unrighteous need to hold her tight and safe for the rest of his life.

Kylie sat up and looped her arms around her bent knees. How could a man's mouth be so sweet and tender and hungry and then become an unrelenting line? "I'm certain you wouldn't know anything about excess sensual energy. How long has *she* been gone—two whole days?"

In the firelight, Michael's grin was slow and devastating. "I told you she was a friend." His tone taunted.

At least he had that, a little jealous spark from her, to comfort his torn nerves.

"What are you doing here, anyway? Why do you always turn up when I'm putting myself together?" But Michael was studying the clearing and Kylie knew he was remembering when her father had brought them both up here. Wary of revealing his hard life, Michael had only been eight to her six, and her father had taught him how to fish. Even then, Michael had known life's hard skills, a boy trying to survive. Poorly fed and clothed, Michael had "made-do" for himself—and not always by legal means. Her parents had both spoken for him when the sheriff came circling him. Those few days away on the camping trip were meant for her alone—Tanner and Miranda didn't want her tagging after them and she'd been hurt. But she didn't mind sharing her father with Michael. Paul Bennett was a gentle man and he'd put his arm around Michael, speaking to him quietly. Michael had tensed, his face paling, but he'd answered, his dark eyes brilliant with unshed tears.

He hadn't known a man like Paul Bennett before, Michael thought, remembering back to the man's calm, easy voice. A man to trust, Paul had been everything in a father that Michael had dreamed of and hadn't had. He'd have given his soul to be Paul Bennett's son, then and always. He hadn't known that fathers could talk so gently, explaining the right and the wrong and the confusion of love and hurt.

Kylie studied Michael's blunt cheekbones, those incredible lashes concealing his thoughts, the tight, wary set of his body. The day they'd come down from the mountain, her father's expression was grim. She'd heard the stories later: her father had been terminally ill, and yet he'd gone to the Cusack shack and called out Fred Cusack. Her father had shamed Fred then, in front of the town, exposing him as a bully. Then he'd turned to Michael. "You can stay with us if you want. You're a good boy. You'll be a fine man. I believe in you. Just keep to the good track and be what a man should be. Keep your pride and your honor," Paul Bennett had said, then he'd walked off, giving Michael his choices.

Her mother had said that Michael stayed with his drunken father because of pride and because he'd known that she—as a widow—could little afford to take him. Fred had died when Michael was eighteen and already gone from Freedom Valley. But he'd returned periodically, and in later years, eventually had been able to replace Fred's charity grave marker with a proper tombstone.

"You can't stay here," Kylie said to Michael, the adult male invading her retreat, as he unrolled his sleeping bag. She resented her mouth watering and her hurry to tear open the box he'd just tossed her, stuffed with raspberry filled pastries. Michael Cusack was an absolute, certified beast, testing her resolve. "This won't get you anywhere," she managed to mumble around a mouthful of delicious pastry. "I'm on a diet. That's why I'm working out."

"I've missed this," he said quietly, stretching his arms high and scanning the stars. "I used to come up here. Your mom packed me lunches and your dad gave me my first fishing pole."

"Well, you probably haven't had time lately. Or energy. After all, you've been too busy with all your women friends." Kylie didn't try to conceal her sarcasm. She swallowed the pastry hard, her heart thumping as she noted how Michael's jeans had slipped a bit on his hips. She looked away into the brush, at a night animal foraging in it. "Leave me alone, Michael."

"Can't. I promised your brother that I'd see you were safe. He's married now, and can't go chasing up mountains at night after you."

"So what are you? My guardian? I'm safe. I've been here hundreds of times before, and alone. I prefer 'alone.' ''

Michael ignored her broad hint and lifted her exercise bra strap on one finger, studying it. "No cups and no hooks. Gray and no lace. What's the world coming to? I remember when Tanner and I wrapped these around the backs of chairs and tried to unhook them without looking."

"I'm sure you've had plenty of practice since then." Kylie grabbed the garment and stuffed it into her sleeping bag.

Michael studied her closely. "My, my, my. You still blush."

"You just came up here to torment me. Go away." Kylie licked the raspberry center from a pastry and Michael inhaled sharply.

The firelight emphasized his tanned face, the unusual dark red glow in his cheeks. "I came because I wanted to give the bears and the cougars a chance to survive... I was worried, okay? I don't like it, but I was."

He rummaged through her utensils, found a skillet and stoked up the fire. From his backpack, he took a wrapped package containing chicken breasts, flopping them onto the olive oil already in the skillet. While they sizzled and the water he placed on the fire was heating, Michael looked directly at her over the campfire. His expression was grim.

"I had a sister. I know what it's like to worry about her. Don't eat too many of those. You need real food."

"I had a peanut butter and grape jelly sandwich.... I didn't know you had a sister."

Michael neatly chopped zucchini squash and added it to the sizzling chicken. "She was a lot older. My mother took Lily with her. I was left with my father. I was only three."

"I can't imagine a mother leaving a child—I know it happens and for good reasons, but I could never— Where is your sister now?"

"Dead. So is my mother. I learned later that she'd had to leave or die, and she'd tried to get me back." Michael's flat tone left no room for more questions, his expression dark and brooding as if an unpleasant memory had just slipped by. He finished preparing the meal, adding cooked linguine to the skillet. They ate quietly, Kylie aware that Michael's thoughts were on his sister.

"You're like your mother," he said when Kylie had helped him wash and dry the utensils. "You understand."

"Some things I do." Kylie grabbed a donut and munched it to keep her mouth busy. Otherwise, she'd attack him for kissing her last night. She didn't want him to think that kiss mattered to her. Michael lay down on his bedroll, and the long length of his body, the memory of it hard against her as they danced, set off her instincts to feast upon him. She swallowed the donut and heard her voice erupt into the night. "I didn't understand that kiss last night, Michael. There was no cause for it. You were either showing off—proving that you still have whatever macho talent that is important to males—or you had missed a night of a sex-fest."

"I was waiting for that. Are you going to sleep in that sweaty getup, or are you cleaning up?"

Kylie leaped to her feet, and instantly her strained muscles protested. "I'm exercising to lose weight, Michael, and you deliberately brought my favorite—"

"You look good," Michael said, but his eyes were drifting over her unbound breasts and the nipples peaking against the cloth. Her body took the impact of that slow gaze, heating and vibrating beneath it.

She looked down at the box of high-priced chocolates that he'd just tossed to her. A jar of raspberry jam followed. He grinned as she held them. "You've got good skills, Kylie. Caught one in each hand."

"I played a lot of softball. And tennis, and handball, and— I don't want to talk with you. You're disrupting my whole thinking-things-out plan." Exercise had momentarily trimmed away her sexual energy, while Leon was using his on her installment-paid massage table. She placed the chocolates and jam carefully by her bedroll, because they were just the thing to savor while she looked at the stars and sorted out her life. She grabbed a towel, washcloth, soap and clean yellow sweat clothes and tramped down to the creek.

When she returned, Michael was still fully dressed, lying upon his bedroll. She tried to ignore his presence and, sitting on her sleeping bag, began her nightly yoga relaxing exercises. Centering into herself, doing the "Child's Pose," the "Dog Pose," and stretching her "sitting bones" and hamstring muscles wasn't quite the same as when she was alone and focused. Michael's presence intruded upon her calm and inner center. His presence flowed warmly, vibrating around her as she bent and stretched and stood.

Muscles stretched, her body feeling better because of the nightly ritual, she slid into her sleeping bag and zipped it. Then, because he was there and because on one level she trusted him, she said, "I think I'm staying in Freedom Valley."

"That's good. It's good here."

"The day you left, you came to Mom's and said you were never coming back. Why did you?"

"I got tired. Anna was special. I called her several times and she must have known how it was with me. She told me it was time to come home. I did, thinking I'd visit with her. I stayed at her house for a while and then bought my place. She was quite a woman."

"She was. Sometimes I talk with her. The house still has the feel of her. Tanner has moved a few of his things and those she wanted him to have into his house, but for the most part, everything is the same," Kylie agreed softly. "I've got to earn money—I'm broke, you know. Leon needed what little money there was left—"

Michael turned to her and blinked. "What?"

"The baby, Michael. They have a baby coming and— I don't hate him, Michael. Leon can't help that he's…well, weak natured. Maybe I am, too, because I've never been a hater—well, except for you. I hated you really well when I was a teenager and you were surfing all the girls. I'm not too certain that I couldn't work up a really good hate for you now."

"Women," he muttered, closed his eyes and shook his head.

"It was my choice. I thought the baby needed a good start. Leon doesn't manage well and Sharon can't manage at all." Kylie waited a while, because her first volley hadn't gone that well. "I like being a massage therapist. I've been doing an amount of it in the retirement home and for my friends—"

Michael turned to her and arched an eyebrow. "The friends you play touch football with?"

"Brody and the rest work hard. Gabriel Deerhorn's neck and shoulders were really aching after breaking that horse.

It took forever to work down his back and his thighs. Then there was Fletcher who hurt his back taking out a window air conditioner and then Koby lifted too many bags of concrete mix and—''

Michael took a long, slow breath as if calming his nerves. He rolled his shoulder and grimaced. His groan was barely audible.

"What's wrong?" Kylie asked, instantly alert to those needing her.

"Nothing."

When he moved painfully, grimacing again, she scrambled out of her sleeping bag. "I think better when my hands are busy. You need a massage to relax. Take off as many clothes as you can so that I can get to you."

"'Get to me,'" he repeated darkly. "It's cold up here. Is freezing my backside off revenge for putting you off when you were fourteen?"

"Sissy. I just wanted to see if steam really came out of a girl's ears when you breathed into them. I'd heard your breathing and tongue could melt bones. I'd even scrubbed my ears five times for the occasion.... Don't worry, you won't feel a thing once I work on you."

"I'd be dead not to," he said flatly, looking at her in that quiet burning way. There was that odd tingling at her nape again as Michael studied her across the campfire, as if he understood what leaped between them and was considering his next move.

"I'll only try to relax you. We won't talk. I don't have my scented oils or music, but it's a peaceful night on the mountain. We'll go with that."

Michael stood slowly, towering over her, the firelight on his face making it seem even more dangerous. His hand rested on his jeans belt, then he tore open the buckle. "Is that what you did with the others? Oil them?"

"Sure," she said, hurriedly turning her back to him as he undressed. A man on a massage table and Michael taking off his clothes were very separate items. "I skipped the tranquillity music and aromatherapy, but Ray had a real sinus thing going and he was glad for the relief."

"I'll bet," Michael muttered darkly. "Ready."

Four

A soft touch and gentle words ease most of what life gives us. The giving eases our own cares.
—Anna Bennett's Journal

"Michael, you're too tense. You've got to give yourself to me," Kylie spoke softly, as Michael lay facedown on his sleeping bag. Her hands gently stroked the taut cords at his neck and shoulders, never leaving his body. Instead of the soothing effect she had explained they would give, her hands skimming his body launched the heavy thrust of his desire. She spoke in cool, professional tones, as though placing herself at a distance from him. "Trust me, Michael. Let the bad energy flow from you. Your back muscles are too tight—too much tension like that can cause a nasty headache. I know we're not in perfect circumstances, but try to relax. Your body is acting defensive. I can't communicate with it. If you'd turn over, I could massage your face.'"

"No." Wearing only his shorts, his arms at his sides, Michael shivered. Cold mountain night air wasn't his immediate problem—it was giving himself to Kylie. Lying on his stomach, his body was warm and tense, particularly in the area of his upper thighs. "Is this what you did for the other ones, York and the rest?"

"No. We managed to use park benches or some arrangement at their houses. Heart or any other kind of problems?"

"None." *But one very large and painful one,* Michael decided.

"Good. I'm going to ask a few questions as we go along, but tell me what you want, what you are feeling. Let me converse with your body." When Michael inhaled abruptly and tensed against the undefined anger curling around him, Kylie said, "Relax, Michael. Think of pleasant things."

Her fingertips smoothed an old scar. "You can tell about these. If they were deep, or there was muscle or tissue damage. I need to know about your body, Michael. There are several round scars. What caused them?"

Michael was silent as Kylie's firm hands gently worked down his legs. Bullet wounds were common in his previous lifestyle, and he didn't want that violence touching Kylie's life.

"I don't suppose they tried anything," he heard himself say, though he'd promised himself not to ask. "At their houses?" he added, resenting his jealousy, now defined as that fiery emotion, and the first bitter taste in his lifetime.

She began to stroke down his backside and then returned to gently rock him with her hands. "Michael. I'm one of the guys. I'm Tanner's little sister. When I'm more settled, I'll probably be taking one of them to the Sweetheart Dance. It's a matter of selection for the long run and getting

to know them as men—changing the parameters of a relationship and getting them to see me as a woman they'd
like to marry. Right now, I'm Anna's daughter and Tanner's sister and I'm divorced. It will take them a while to
adjust to me as an adult and a single woman. They're all
just excellent dancers and I haven't danced in years. Leon
was too muscle-bound—he moved rather stiffly. They were
all very sweet and actually cooperated a lot more than you
are doing…. And besides I know touch points that can
momentarily paralyze a difficult client. You've got to flow
with this, Michael—give yourself to me,'' she repeated ear-
nestly.

He wanted to give himself to her forever. He wanted to
stake his claim, show her how much he adored her, how
much he wanted to—to bond with her. The primitive need
shocked him and Michael shivered. ''Did that happen often—a difficult customer?''

''Mmm. Once or twice. It's an occupational hazard.
Word gets around and then I wasn't bothered again. You're
too tense for this. Your hands are in fists at your sides—
that will never do. Let's try this. It's compensating for the
lack of a massage bench, but you need to feel warm and
safe. You're big enough and sturdy enough to hold my
weight.'' Kylie hesitated, then eased to lie over Michael's
back. She rested her chin on his shoulder. Her hands
stroked his arms. ''Maybe it's because it's so cold here. I'll
keep you warm…. There. Just relax. You're warm and snug
and secure.''

Michael knew exactly about his desire to be warm and
about his need for secure, tight, soft places. Kylie began to
hum gently against his ear. The soft sound saturated desire
into every cell of his body. He tried to concentrate on not
rolling over and taking her mouth. He tried to deflect his
attention, which had fully focused on Kylie's lush mouth

beside his ear and her body warm over his, the gentle rub of her breasts against his back. He felt like purring, the emotion stunning him. He realized that with Kylie anything could happen—he just wasn't certain of what and when and how much he could leash himself with her. That shocked Michael's concept of himself as controlled and remotely cool. "What was that you said about staying in Freedom Valley and earning money?"

She spoke quietly, "If I had a place, I'd open a business. I'd call it 'Soft Touches.' No one has taken Mom's place, not really, with her scented soaps and candles and home remedies. When I didn't have appointments, I could work on those things. I want to make homemade jam, too, and take it to the neighbors just as she used to do. I want to grow flowers and visit those who need me. I'd like to do that here, in Freedom Valley. I'm enjoying Mom's place too much, but I'd like to keep my business away from there. Tanner said I could use a corner of his boat crafting business which is next door to Mom's, but I don't know. I do know that I like the values in the men here, and I want a family. I want what Mom had, the security of Freedom and neighbors who care, of children growing up together. Somewhere in the Bachelor Club there could be a husband for me, someone I'd like to court and marry and have those babies—three, I think…I'm not supposed to be the one who is talking. Just concentrate on relaxing."

Michael didn't want to think about her sifting through the requirements of a husband amid the Bachelor Club. He could see her customers lining up, working on Tanner's wooden boats and waiting in line for Kylie's knowledge-able fingers. He resented the urge to keep her close and safe and her hands off other men. "I've got plenty of room at my electric shop in town. I use it mostly for storage, but the front part could be converted into what you want. I'm away a lot, so you'll have the place to yourself. We could deduct the price of regular massages from the rent. I strain a few muscles now and then, and you're right, I'm too tense.''

Kylie's fingers skimmed down to his shoulders and he stiffened as they dug into the tense muscle. "Knots there.... You mean you're away a lot—with your women?''

Just that nick of her temper took him over the edge. Michael turned and rolled Kylie beneath him. He glanced down the length of their bodies, his bare legs fitted between the legs of Kylie's sweatpants. Then he studied her stunned expression, the sudden desire darkening her eyes. The mountain's night air seemed to crackle between them like bolts of dancing electricity. He placed his hand on the soft, warm curve of her cheek and whispered, "I haven't had a woman in years, Kylie. Does that shock you?''

"Why not?'' she whispered back, the sound intimate and soft and feminine as he knew she would sound on her wedding bed, when she was gently worn by life.

"Maybe I've been waiting for you.'' The truth tore out of him into the crisp night air, and he waited for her reaction.

"I don't believe you one minute. You're not a waiting man,'' she whispered unevenly. "You see. You want. You take.''

"With you, yes. I'd like that. But maybe I'd like to be courted like other men. Maybe I'm sensitive and old-fashioned.'' Michael lowered his mouth to hers, brushing the softness lightly. *Dreams,* he mused, *she tastes of dreams.*

She arched to his hand as it slid to cover the fabric over her breast. "I can't think—you're too close. You've always done that to me, sucked away my ability to think.''

He smiled slowly, aware of her trembling warm body,

of the needs racing through her. He settled closer, placing his lips against her throat and kissing her fragrant silky skin. "Go with the flow, wasn't that what you said? Don't think. Relax, just as you told me to do."

Her fingertips dug into his shoulders, her eyes wide and shadowed in her pale face, a frothing mist of curls surrounding it. Her lips looked soft and dewy and just right—and her lids closed as he lowered his head.

As he gently nibbled her lobe, Kylie tensed. Her arms shot around his neck and held him tight, and the surge of her hips against the hardness of his startled him. "Kylie?" he asked, uncertain of himself, of his reactions to her.

"Michael...." Her husky appeal and warm, flushed cheek against his shattered him. He lay very still, braced upon her smaller softer body and listened to the heavy thump of their hearts as if they were meant to march together through life.

Kylie's hands smoothed his shoulders, not in the massage as she had before, but in the way a woman's hands could gently tether a man forever. When her fingertips smoothed his cheeks, he turned to kiss her palm, and then her eyes were soft upon him. "You're afraid, aren't you?" she whispered.

"Maybe." None of this should be happening. Not with Kylie. He could hurt her.

"Why?"

He closed his eyes and her fingertips gently caressed his lashes. He could have spent a lifetime under her hands, all his shadowy past purged by her light touch.

"Don't be so harsh on yourself."

He smiled against her fingertips as they cruised lightly over his lips. "You sound like your mother."

Her warm touch stopped and hovered above his lips. "But I'm not. I'm me."

"That's the problem, dreamy-eyes," Michael murmured and knew he had to ease away from her. Kylie in a soft, feminine mood, or in a playful or angry one could entice him, drawing uncertain emotions from him—like tenderness and the thought that he'd cherished her all his life. The imprint of her soft, warm body stayed with him as he stood. One look down at Kylie's pale, mysterious expression and Michael grabbed a towel from his backpack. He strode for safety—the icy water of the creek.

Splashing himself with water, he was just damning himself thoroughly, for wanting her so desperately, for wanting to place his hands intimately upon her—wanting to taste her skin, her breasts, to lose himself in her sweetness. "Selfish bastard," he muttered to himself in the cold night. "You've got enough of your old man in you to take what you want. Keep your hands to yourself."

The brush bordering the creek rustled and Kylie stepped into view. With her hands on her hips and a toss of her head, she glared at him. "You always did that—run away. Is that what you do with your women? What's the matter? Aren't I up to your standards?"

Michael returned the glare. "You're not one of my women. You don't qualify. Get that straight."

"You make me so mad that I could just jump you and hold your head underwater until a little of that arrogance washes away."

"You and who else? I outweigh you by seventy-five pounds and a whole lot of experience."

"I've learned a bit since we were young, Mr. Hot Stuff."

Michael shook his head. Kylie had never walked away from a fight and he promised himself he wasn't giving her one—or anything else. Holding her furious glare, he stepped out of the creek, grabbed his towel and dried roughly. On his way past her, he threw the towel at her.

He was just calling himself an idiot, snapping his jeans and wondering what he was doing on a chilly night splashing in a freezing creek when Kylie marched past him. She dropped the damp towel from her fingertips like he suspected she wanted to drop any association with him.

She began to roll her sleeping bag, complete with the rosebud splattered pillow. Kylie, in a mood, was capable of doing anything. Michael didn't trust her. Or himself. "What are you doing?" he asked in a voice he hoped was calm.

"Leaving."

The mountain trail was treacherous during daylight; at night it was too dangerous. The mountain's chill sank into Michael's heart. "Not now. In the morning."

Kylie straightened and glared at him. "I'll take the offer of the shop, because it's close to town and practical. But I won't be ordered by you."

"Now, honey," Michael managed to say, as images of Kylie's torn and bruised body slammed into him. "Be reasonable. It's dangerous to go down the path in the dark."

"You just called me 'honey.' Is that what you call your women?" she demanded hotly as she tore a flashlight out of her backpack.

Michael knew he was holding on, clinging by his fingertips over a deep dark chasm. He struggled for logic, but it wasn't easy after "honey" had just leaped out of his lips. Still stunned, his instincts told him that he'd been hoarding his endearments for Kylie. He remembered then how Paul Bennett had called Anna "dear heart." Uncertain what to say while his unfamiliar emotions were churning, Michael decided for a verbal shrug-off. "It's a term men use."

"So it means nothing. Just like that kiss at the dance. Like when you were so tender a moment ago," she rapped accusingly at him. "You're afraid of tenderness and intimacy. Big bad Michael Cusack is afraid of meaningful conversation and relationships other than those he has with his women.''

''Could we leave this nowhere conversation and get into a sane one?'' he asked warily.

Kylie stood immobile and he wasn't certain what she would do next. ''Okay,'' she said finally, and unrolled her sleeping bag. She kicked off her shoes, crawled into it and ripped the zipper upward. She crossed her arms as if the matter were ended. ''Deal. We talk about something else. Do you agree?''

With a nod and a sigh of relief, Michael crouched to add more wood to the fire. He could just feel safety lurk nearby when Kylie said, ''I want to know why you didn't play team sports like the rest of the guys. All through school, you would shoot baskets at our house, and that hoop is still over Mom's old garage. You were good. You hit homers in the cow pasture baseball, and yet you never played on the school teams. I heard from the guys that you're still good.''

Kylie had been unpredictable when she was younger, but now as a woman, she was as volatile as an ungrounded electric wire. He wasn't certain he liked the feeling that she could reach into him and grab his heart in her small fist. Michael studied her. ''Maybe it was a matter of money. Track shoes cost, so do the rest.''

''Bunk and double bunk. I know how hard you worked to support your father until he died. You've always worked, either in town or on the ranches, and you had money.''

''Girls, Sherlock. Dating costs.''

''So did Tanner's track shoes—the ones *you* bought and hung on Mom's back porch. So did the ribbons and the other things, like Mom's little leather manicure set. You knew she never would have treated herself to that and that there was no money for Tanner's sports supplies or those little gold studs I wanted when I was fifteen. You bought Mom a good set of leather gloves when her hands were torn picking blackberries in the bramble. I still have the earrings and the gold locket you gave me when I turned sixteen by the way. Karolina picked up most of it—she was always good at details, even when we were kids—and I saw you from my bedroom window the night you left Tanner's track shoes. You were lucky I didn't shoot you with my slingshot. I was pretty good then. Karolina has apparently forgotten all her early sleuth work. I haven't.''

Michael studied Kylie and knew she was out to terrorize him. ''Are you done?''

''No. I'll tell you when I am.'' She glared at him for a moment and then said, ''I'm done.''

Michael considered the woman who had just turned her back to him, sealing him away from her. Helpless wasn't an emotion he'd had since he was a child and now it circled him. He badly wanted to pick her up and hold her and cuddle her. Kylie flipped back over, catching his tender expression before he could wipe it away. To protect himself and her, Michael stated darkly, ''Don't pull the do-gooder act with me. Don't try to push me into something I'm not. It won't work.''

''You're afraid,'' she cooed, unafraid and taunting him. Then she shifted that luscious mobile mouth into a smirk and murmured, ''Gotcha.''

Michael found himself grinning. ''Exactly what would the Women's Council say if they knew we were spending the night together—again?''

Kylie's smirk died. ''You know good and well that the traditions of Freedom Valley are that if a couple spends the night together, the man is expected to go before the Council and present himself as a proper bridegroom candidate. It

isn't necessary, but it's a custom that every woman really
wants, no matter how modern she is. Our mothers and
grandmothers have wanted the same, and were courted according to custom. I can't see you doing that. You've been
a Cull too long. You have all those women. You're a legend
in your own time, a heartthrob of every girl when we were
younger. You wouldn't do that just to embarrass me, like
that kiss on the dance floor, would you?''

''Wouldn't I?'' Michael watched her digest exactly what
he could do, and slid into his sleeping bag.

''You know that if you speak for me, it will stop other
men from asking me for casual dates. You're just contrary
enough to— I really need a date, Michael, so don't do that.
I'm determined to—'' Kylie lifted up on one elbow and
scowled at him. ''Never mind. Just don't interfere with my
life.''

''Mmm,'' he returned blandly, not giving Kylie the reassurance that she wanted. He looked up at the stars
through the pine branches and savored Kylie's silent frustration, the rustling of her sleeping bag as she flip-flopped
in it and the punching of her pillow. After a time, he heard
her sigh; her light breathing changed into a slow, steady
rhythm. Kylie, sleeping nearby, settled the dark shadows
prowling around Michael's heart and he gave himself to
the gentle sound.

Used to living in dangerous places, Michael awoke instantly, aware that in the predawn, something approached
him—his first thought was for the safety of Kylie and of
the cougars and wolves known to hunt upon the mountains.
Then he caught Kylie's earthy scent, mingled with sweet
violets and he looked up into her face. He answered the
unspoken question hovering on her lips—''No, they
weren't my children. To father a child is a serious respon-

sibility, a life to cherish. I haven't considered children, but I know I'd want to be there for them. Go back to sleep."

"Tough guy," Kylie mocked gently in the darkness. Then she bent to kiss his forehead. "Good night."

That light kiss, like a mother to a child, would burn Michael's skin for hours later. She'd be giving kisses like that to her children one day and then she'd be going to bed with her husband. "Kylie?" he asked as she settled into her sleeping bag.

"Umm?"

"Don't ever go to a man in the middle of the night."

"Why not?"

"Just don't," he managed finally as his body ached with the need to hold her close.

Early the next afternoon, too filled with restless images of her night with Michael and her plans for Soft Touches, Kylie began to wash and starch—one of her mother's recommended "problem-solvers." She'd washed blankets and hung them on her mother's wire clothesline to dry in the bright Montana autumn. While the blankets were drying, she'd hauled the old tin washtubs out of the garage and filled them for the hand-stitched quilts that needed more tender care. The two huge tubs sat in her mother's backyard, exactly as Kylie had remembered, the autumn sunlight filtering through the fiery leaves of the old oak tree. "A good soak in soap and soda, a few swishes, and sunshine, that's all good quilts need," her mother had said.

Dressed in a sweatshirt and jeans, Kylie gently eased Magda Claas's hand-stitched quilt into the warm water. One of the Founding Mothers and Kylie's ancestor, Magda was a butter maker, a midwife and a healer, just as Anna had been.

Kylie surveyed her mother's yard, autumn leaves drifting

across the sleeping beds of peonies, lavender, tulips and irises. In the summer, Anna's yard was a multicolored fiesta of flowers, the herbs' scents fragrantly blending with the magnolia blooms. Kylie had needed this healing place, with good loving memories in which to rest, before moving on with her life. She'd ordered catalogs for aromatherapy, massage benches and electric devices to relax overly taut muscles.

When an image of Michael from this morning sliced into her brain, his rugged jaw covered with morning stubble, and his black eyes searing her, Kylie plunged her elbows into the soapy water, swishing the treasured quilts. At the campsite, he'd cooked breakfast, a delicious skillet of bacon and eggs and hash browns and then had slathered a biscuit with butter, placing it against her lips. ''Eat,'' he'd ordered grimly. ''The sooner we're off the mountain, the better. And if you know what's good for you, don't do any more of those yoga exercises.''

Kylie washed the quilt gently, remembering Michael's gaze as it drifted to the butter on her lips. His stormy expression had darkened as she licked her bottom lip. ''What's it to you?'' she'd asked, just to set him off, just to pry him from his grim mood.

''This,'' he'd answered darkly and bent to place his lips against hers. The kiss was light and easy, as if he were cherishing her, but the electric current leaped, snagged and locked onto her immediately. The jolt shot down her body, skittered up her back and she'd placed the plate aside, her heart pounding as Michael studied her. He shook his head. ''You're too sweet, Kylie. Everything you're thinking is written on your face.''

''And? What am I thinking?'' *She'd wanted to grab him and have him, and treasure him.*

When he was silent, his hand wrapped around hers, Kylie closed her eyes. She'd held his hand tightly, until he drew away. "I'm thinking," she'd said, lying to herself and to him, to cover the need to rest against him, "that I came up here to think and that if you hadn't been such a rat last night, I would have given myself a fantastic pedicure. I would have felt much better this morning with beautiful feet. If I could teach someone in this town reflexology, I would. Karolina's hands are too small and weak. It's her brain that's big and strong."

Michael had been too quiet, waves of his personal vibrant energy washing over her. He'd looked at her sock-covered feet and had grimly pushed her boots over them. He tied the lashes briskly. "Not me. Not your feet," he stated roughly.

"Was I asking you, in particular?" she'd shot at him, because her feet were perfectly fine.

"I could make you ask, and we both know it," he had replied slowly, and the clear air scented of pines and earth swirled mysteriously around Kylie. That curious prickling ran up her spine and danced on her skin.

Now, in her mother's backyard, with the quilt wet, bulky and heavy in her hands, Kylie wrung it gently. She eased it into the rinse water. Years ago, she used to hold one end as her mother twisted the quilts, wringing them before rinsing.

Kylie closed her eyes as a van and cars pulled into her mother's driveway. There was no mistaking Fidelity Moore, Dahlia Greer, Jasmine Thatcher and Sadie McGinnis as they emerged, sighting her instantly and making their way for her.

"You didn't wring out the soap water enough before putting it into the rinse tub," ninety-year-old Fidelity Moore stated crisply. "That will never do. Put the quilt back into the soapy water and change the rinse water."

The metallic flash on the road in front of Anna's blinded Kylie momentarily, then she recognized Michael's service truck. It had passed the driveway and was backing up. It

pulled up slowly beside the van and cars. Michael got out,
shot her a pinning, assessing look that set her pulse racing,
and she prayed he'd leave. Instead he opened the side panels to retrieve his tool belt and strapped it on as if she were
a customer. He walked toward the women, a tall man with
shaggy black hair, broad shoulders and long powerful legs,
enough male confection to suck the breath from any
woman. "Good afternoon, ladies," he said, nodding to
them.

"Fuse box," Kylie explained hurriedly. "Old wiring.
Dad did a good job, but the wire covering is crumbling and
Michael is just—"

"Hold there, young man," Fidelity's aged but firm voice
called out as Michael began up the back steps.

Michael stopped and stiffened. Kylie's body turned cold.
Fidelity's "Hold there" command had been known to
freeze charging bulls. Then Michael turned to smile that
devastatingly beautiful, charming, woman-catching smile,
and came down the steps. "I don't think Michael has time
to spare," Kylie said, uncertain about how he would react
to the pounding questions certain to come. "He has another
job, but the fire hazard to Mom's house—"

"I've plenty of time," Michael said, watching her as
Kylie began to twist the old quilt. As if he were used to
the task, Michael pulled up his sweatshirt sleeves, stripped
off his workman's belt and put it on the old picnic table.
He took the wet quilt from her hands and twisted it gently,
plopping it onto the backyard picnic table. He frowned at
the soapy rinse water and noted, "You didn't get enough
of the wash water out. Anna was very careful about that."

"I know, I know, I know," Kylie muttered. In another
moment, the Women's Council would be reminding her of
Michael's Cull status.

"Take very good care of her doilies, Kylie," Fidelity
ordered. "If you need your mother's sugar-starch recipe

and help on how to form the ruffles, call me. Your mother taught me. Some of the doilies and designs came down from Magda Claas, your ancestor and excellent with a crochet hook. So was your mother. You've always been so much on the move that I doubt Anna could keep you still long enough to embroider pillowcases for your hope chest...."

Fidelity's aged blue gaze burned through the mid-October air to pin Kylie. "You do have a hope chest, don't you? It's one of the requirements for a bride hereabouts."

"It's upstairs," Kylie answered, feeling as if she were in the third grade instead of a woman who had run a business and had managed a household with a husband not carrying his share. "I didn't take it with me when I married."

"You should have abided by the customs of Freedom Valley and your first marriage would have been solid. But then, the young and foolish make mistakes, don't we all?"

"Could be." Kylie had already acknowledged her marital mistakes—she'd given too much to Leon. He hadn't given enough—or wanted to.

Fidelity wasn't backing off. "Do you want to marry again?"

"I'll just dump this," Michael said, attaching a hose to the tin rinse tub and draining the water from it into Anna's old peony bed. "Be right back with clean rinse water."

Fidelity's alert gaze considered Michael. "You're a Cull, aren't you, boy?"

Michael grinned at her. "Have been. I'd change if the right woman came along."

"We can't have you run amok, contaminating all the good work we've done with the men here in Freedom Valley," Fidelity stated firmly. "You'll have to change your ways."

"Yes, ma'am. I'm considering it." Michael's grin blazed in the dappled shadows of Anna's backyard, and Kylie stared at him blankly, trying to align the woman-hunting boy with the man who stood beside her, as solid and true as any man in Freedom Valley. He had the same stance as her father did, boots planted firmly upon the fallen leaves, a man giving his word and intending to keep it.

"Hmm. Just here to do the wiring, you say," Dahlia purred. A woman who enjoyed men, Dahlia noted Michael's taut jean-covered backside as he took two buckets and went into Anna's house for hot water.

Fidelity settled upon the picnic table and studied Kylie. "He used to do that for Anna," she said. "Rogue that he is, Michael Cusack can be a gentleman. Anna used to go to his house, especially when his women were visiting. I want to hear what the boy has to say for himself," Fidelity stated in her President of the Women's Council tone. When Michael returned, she asked, "You know the girl is skitterish around you and you know why, don't you?"

Michael met Fidelity's gaze. "Yes, ma'am. I do."

"She's a fine girl. A little headstrong and sometimes acts without caution. You can go along now and get more rinse water. I like to see a man washing quilts."

Kylie crossed her arms. "If you're talking about me, I have a thing or two to say. First of all, I'm not skitterish. Not in the least."

Michael's teasing finger at her nape startled her and Fidelity smiled fondly at him. He made two more trips for hot water, then plopped the end of the quilt into Kylie's hands. He twisted the other end of quilt gently and eased it into the fresh rinse water. Picking up another quilt from the basket, he eased it into the wash water. "There," he said, drying his hands on his sweatshirt and smiling charmingly at the women. "I'd be happy to help any of you with your electrical work, or with quilt washing."

Fidelity sniffed elegantly. "That's a start. If you stay on

the straight and narrow, I'll see what can be done about removing you from the Cull bin.''

"I'd be grateful, ma'am. I'll try.''

Kylie could have killed him. Michael knew as well as she that the women had come to investigate his intentions. "Nothing is going on,'' she said flatly to the women she'd known since birth.

"Two nights,'' Fidelity stated crisply. "One here and one up on the mountain.''

"What are your sources?'' Kylie asked and nudged Michael, who had come to stand beside her. He wasn't providing logical explanations why they'd been together. She glared up at him and blinked, for Michael had never looked so innocent.

"Michael's black four-wheeler parked beside your white little truck along the path leading up to the mountain. They were there all night, intimately side by side, a rendezvous in the mountains,'' Sadie stated haughtily.

"Car trouble?'' Kylie managed to provide without much sincerity.

"There's no need to conceal facts, not from us. We're only concerned about the unmarried, and maintenance of the married women here in Freedom Valley. Tanner, your brother, said you needed protection. Michael offered. He's helpful that way, aren't you, Michael?'' Fidelity asked quietly. "Thank you for fixing my radio. It's very dear to me, a gift from my dear departed Alfonso.''

Her wise blue gaze brushed Kylie's flushed face. Then Fidelity slowly studied Michael's expression, the way he stood close and protectively beside Kylie. The way he took her hand and met Fidelity's gaze evenly. "Yes,'' the older woman said quietly, as if she had settled the matter in her mind. "I think we should be going now. It's clear to me that Michael is only taking care of Kylie because of his love for Anna. Kylie, dear, do put me on your massage list.

Henry at the retirement home says you do wonders with your hands, just like your mother's herbal teas and ointments used to do. Come along, girls. We've got work to do. I'm certain that if Michael ever decides to court a woman, he'd ask for The Rules for Bride Courting. You'll do that, won't you, Michael?''

"But he's a Cull," Sadie protested hurriedly. "He's impregnated so many women that—"

"Michael assured me that those were not his babies, and that those women were his friends. I believe him," Kylie stated firmly. She didn't know why she believed Michael, but she'd trusted her heart and her instincts all her life. She gripped Michael's large callused hand tighter when he would have moved away. She would protect him, even if his hackles were rising and he was withdrawing into a protective, cold shield.

"You stand by him, then?" Fidelity pushed.

"I do."

"You are very much like your mother. The world needs people who are soft and loving and believing. There are people who take advantage of a kind heart, but not Michael. There was a time that Kylie's father came to me and though he knew he wouldn't be long for the world, he spoke to me of Michael. Paul spoke as a father fond of a son, smoothing the path for when he was gone. From time to time, good men speak up for their sons and Paul spoke for Michael. Time…that is what this is all about. Come along, girls," Fidelity stated crisply while Dahlia's knowing chuckle floated on the autumn air. "Michael, you'll be very careful with Kylie—I mean with her mother's quilts, won't you?"

"Yes, ma'am," Michael agreed firmly, as if taking another vow.

"Good boy. You may kiss my cheek now—and don't

worry, Sadie. I'm past the age of conceiving from a kiss, or anything more likely.''

When the women were gone, Michael studied Kylie. Her eyes were bright with anger, sunlight shooting a halo of sparks around her head, the tendrils dancing in the autumn breeze. With the old patchwork quilts strung on the line behind her, she looked sweet and hot and volatile, glaring at him. He wished he could pick her up and twirl her around and listen to her laughter. Yet, he reconsidered, simmering suited her, too. He couldn't resist teasing her. ''You're blushing. Do you know how fascinating that is?''

''If you ever—'' she began a threat that died when Michael's lips brushed hers.

''I can't decide whether your eyes now are glittering like blue topaz or sunlight on the clearest blue stream. When they're wide and clear and blue as the Montana sky, a man could give his soul to have you look at him.''

She stared at him and tried to align the romantic phrasing and Michael's hard mouth, now curved with humor. ''Huh?''

He lifted her chin with his thumb and studied her while her heart stopped and flopped and her blood surged wildly through her trembling body. ''That's it then. For me,'' he said before brushing a light kiss over her lips. ''What's next? The sheets?''

What's next? What's next? That night the words ran through Kylie's mind as she lay alone, tossing in her lonely bed. She held a pillow against her for comfort, then flopped over on it, just as she'd wanted to pin Michael to the earth and kiss him.

As she was drifting off to sleep, she thought she heard her mother's soft laughter.

Five

I've often told my children of the value of soft touches, of the healing that hands can do for the body and for the spirit. My Kylie has a gift that needs sharing.
—Anna Bennett's Journal

The third week of October, Kylie opened Soft Touches. After a hectic week, her massage therapy business had been installed into the large shop at the front of Michael's 1880s building. With his friends, Tanner—a carpenter—had split the area into a waiting room, a therapy room and a bathroom. For a free massage amid the noise and the rubble, Ollie Liefstrom had painted the big front window with an 1880s-style scrolling bold, Soft Touches. Dorothy Polson donated the blinds from her refurbished beauty shop to add privacy for waiting customers. A temporary loan from Tanner and Gwyneth financed the town's required business license, the massage bench and basic supplies.

The first three days Soft Touches was open, Kylie worked from early morning until evening, and then dragged herself home. That third night, she slowly, achingly got out of her pickup and trudged up the steps. She shoved open the door, entered and then walked back out. "Where've you been?" she asked the tall man sprawled on her mother's front porch swing. "Check with me tomorrow, and I'll work you into my schedule. I need the deduction from the rent money I owe you."

She stepped back inside to close the door; Michael's big workman's boot prevented the door from closing. He pushed a large paper sack marked Wagon Wheel Café into her hands. He added a small white sack from Eli's Bakery. While she was dealing with the delicious aroma, he smoothed the tousled curls back from her face and smiled gently down at her. "Tired?"

Michael and good food from Willa's Wagon Wheel Café and Eli's pastries were too much even when she wasn't tired. Kylie nodded and wanted to lean against him, just to let him hold her. "Thanks," she said and wondered why just looking at him took her breath away. All her tired muscles seemed to tense, and her heart started flip-flopping wildly. "Where have you been? I haven't seen much of you."

She'd seen him when the aroma of his slow cooker soup pot beckoned. There always seemed to be an extra sandwich for her and Michael apparently loved morning pastry with his coffee. "Eat 'em before they get old," he'd said, tossing her one before going back to his work.

"I'm rewiring that old Jenkins house." Michael had explained little in his lifetime. Yet she sensed that explaining his whereabouts to her was important to him.

"That's not all you've been up to. Winter is coming and people are busy with fix-up work. I heard you do free work at the retirement home. Talk is that with all the free work you do and the way you live, you must have an outside income. Rewiring Macy's chicken brooder house should have cost more than a few eggs and an occasional chicken dinner. And repairing the Fines' milking machines wasn't easy. You could have charged."

"Hey. Free milk, cheese, buttermilk and eggs. A guy has to eat, and when I want my pick of the cat or dog litters, they're free," Michael returned with a shrug. He studied her in that wary, assessing and quiet way. "You're driving yourself too hard."

"I like work. It's what I need now." She needed to give ease, and thus help herself mend. She'd worked past the allotted schedule with Blanche Loring, who had wrenched her back lifting a bale of hay. The woman's tight muscles needed relaxing and she'd hugged Kylie gratefully. That hug was enough pay for the extra time.

Michael's finger prowled through the tendrils around her ears. "Take it easy, Kylie. You can't solve everything in a few days."

The sacks crackled in Kylie's tightening fists. He'd kissed her hungrily, placed his hand upon her breast and a river of emotion swept through her. On one hand, she wanted him in her bed. On the other, she wanted to understand her emotions for him. She wanted to understand why he had kissed her so desperately and so tenderly. Michael acquired few attachments and his touch left little doubt that she appealed to him sensually. His body had been too tight and lean and hot to deny that attraction. *She would not be one of his women.* "You've never had a pet that I know of. Your horse is practical, isn't he? That's why you have him?"

He nodded and Kylie sensed that Michael's life had twisted over many dark paths. He wasn't a man for companionship or warmth, preferring his solitude. He gave little of himself and yet he stood in her mother's house, offering her food. The chilly autumn wind had whipped his hair, and her fingers ached to smooth the thick, black strands. His jacket collar was turned up and loneliness stirred in the shadows enfolding him. She scanned the hard planes of his face, the shadows around his deep-set eyes. She wanted to wrap her arms around him and hold him tight. "Don't tell me about where you get your income. I don't want to know."

The scars on Michael's body weren't ordinary, especially the slash across his forearm. The tiny white lines down his back had been barely recognizable in the light of the campfire, but Kylie remembered her father cutting up Michael's father's belt. Her father had been furious then, his uncustomary display of angry frustration frightening her.

Michael recognized her look, those wide blue eyes searching his face; he couldn't be one of her orphans, dragged in from the cold. He didn't want Kylie's sympathy.

He's lonely, she thought, and missing my mother. Michael shrugged, still studying her and she didn't understand the warmth swirling around her. "Get some sleep, dear heart," he said before brushing a kiss across her lips. The light, electric connection of their mouths dived into her blood and made it zing. *Dear heart,* the tender name her father had given her mother.

"You're not going anywhere," she said firmly, and resented the lips that spoke before her brain circled the dangers of Michael within grabbing distance. She resented the hand that shot to his jacket and prevented him from leaving her. When Michael's dark gaze slowly took in her pale fist and followed it up her arm to her throat and then to her lips and then to her eyes, Kylie shivered. She uncurled her fingers from his jacket, dug into Eli's pastries and bit into a raspberry filled bismark. "Come in."

Michael followed her into the kitchen and when Kylie placed the sacks on the table, he eased her coat from her and removed the second pastry from her mouth, placing it aside. "You're working too hard. You've got circles under your eyes, and you're not eating right."

"Same to you. You don't look any better." Kylie plopped two plates and silverware onto her mother's kitchen table where many serious life decisions had been made. "Take off your coat and sit down. I'm running this show. Gwyneth, Tanner's wife, told me about his little chat with you and the rest of his friends—my friends, who are on my schedule right now and good paying customers. My brother takes his position seriously, but I am capable of making my own decisions. There's gossip already about you and me—"

Michael sat slowly, unpacking the food from the sack. The lock of his jaw, the stiff set of his shoulders, the methodical unpeeling and folding of the tinfoil covering the dishes spoke of his thoughtful mood. "Does it bother you?"

"Of course not. I know that nothing is happening between us. But sharing the same building, we need to establish basic rules. Do not glare at my men customers."

He leveled a dark look at her. "Maybe I've got a reason."

"Maybe you don't—oh, yum! Willa's shrimp alfredo and salad. Yummy, yummy, yummy." On impulse, because right then her life was full and good—she had a good start on a business she loved, she had good food to eat, and because she had Michael across the dinner table from her— Kylie leaned over to kiss him. "Thanks."

"Is that all it takes—food?" he asked warily as she ate. A sensual quiver played around him and he tried not to stare as she licked her lips and closed her eyes in delight. He wanted her eyes open the first time they made love, filling with him....

"Yum," was all Kylie could say gratefully, looking at him as she ate a sugarcoated donut. With his dark shaggy hair tousled by the wind and a maroon sweater and jeans, he looked delicious. She noted that his jaw was gleaming, as though recently shaven. The morning on the mountain when he was grumpy, his jaw had been dark with stubble, his expression stormy. Either way, she wanted to place her hand on his cheek and soothe whatever ran dark and troubled inside him. "Thanks."

"Sure. Anytime." Then he leaned over to lick her bottom lip. He smiled as the jolt shot through her, the need to leap upon him. "You had powdered sugar on your lips. Do you always dive into everything, racing through it, like you just did dinner?"

The underlying question could have been anything, but at the moment, kissing Michael was on Kylie's mind. The past few relaxed moments were blasted away by the electricity charging through her. "What's happening, Michael?"

His dark simmering look had frightened her. "Leon didn't like sexually aggressive women. Do you?" she blurted out and wondered why. She wondered what he would do if she kissed him as she wanted, put her hands on him as she wanted...tore his sweater off as she wanted and his jeans and—but she wouldn't.

"An active woman is preferred." Michael continued to study her. "Come here," he whispered, taking her hand to draw her onto his lap. "Afraid?" he asked when she resisted, perching stiffly on his lap.

''I ache in every muscle possible,'' she whispered as he nuzzled her throat, those hard lips warm and open upon her skin. She arched when his big warm hand found and kneaded the knots on her shoulders.

''You're working too hard.'' Michael loved how she fitted his hands, how her body flowed to his stroke. He'd given ease to the women he'd been with, but he'd remained detached, giving only enough for relief. Now, with Kylie, he wondered what it would be like to touch her every day like this, to tend her, to listen to those long, pleasured sighs. He swallowed roughly, unfamiliar with those tender emotions, uncertain and awash in them. He'd kept himself apart for years and the incredible tearing sensation of his heart stunned him.

''Sleepyhead,'' he whispered tenderly against her lips. ''You're barely keeping your eyes open. Why don't you take a shower and go to bed? I'll do the dishes.''

''I couldn't—''

''Sure, you can. You can do anything you want.''

''Do you really think so, Michael?'' She searched his face to see if he was mocking her.

''I do.'' Michael's tone was just as firm as if he were taking a vow. His dark eyes were soft and warm upon her, just as her father's gaze had considered her mother.

''Michael?'' Kylie gave way to the need to smooth his hair. He held very still beneath her touch. ''Why did you buy that building on the square? It's old like the rest, and you've had to repair so much, the old adobe outer walls worn by weather. You've got a storage building at your place and you have only a few things in the back room.''

He shrugged again and his expression closed as he looked away. ''Poker parties?''

Kylie's hand smoothed his hair and Michael held oddly still. She considered how this powerful man needed petting and cuddling and how his beautiful soulful eyes met hers. "Try this. You wanted to preserve the building for its history. If you hadn't bought it, it would have been demolished for a parking lot. That's an awful lot of money, Michael, and no one really knows all the good you do, do they? You're uncomfortable with that—the good in you. Don't be."

His mouth firmed as he looked at her. "There are women like you, who believe in good and honor that just isn't there. Life isn't always a fairy tale for them."

"Mmm. Stop trying to be such a tough guy."

"You never stop, do you? Believing? Dreaming?"

"Nope. I had a rough bump in life, but I believe." Kylie closed her eyes as Michael's lips came closer, lightly brushing hers.

The next day, Michael couldn't force his thoughts from Kylie. He wasn't pushing her too soon; he would be very careful with her. She was Anna's daughter and she was basically untouched, uncertain of herself as a woman. She needed time to adjust to her life, to take it back. Michael cursed her ex-husband for that damage.

He cursed the luring scent of oranges and the gentle music coming from the front part of his building. He wondered who was relaxing beneath Kylie's knowing hands. There was no real reason for him to be here; he had what he needed in his truck. Yet he wanted to be close to her, to hear her voice, to hear that gurgling husky laughter suddenly burst through the shadows like sunshine. She'd laugh if she knew how much care he took to see that she had lunch, making more food than he could eat. Since she'd opened the shop, he'd hurried to Eli's Bakery. Carrying out a sack filled with raspberry bismarks, Michael ignored the baker's broad knowing grin. "I got my wife with an apple pie. When you want the recipe, let me know."

In the shop, Michael had worried over the arrangement of the pastries, trying for an artful careless look, just to hear Kylie's delighted morning "Yum."

He wasn't a match for emotionally wide-open and trusting Kylie. Around her, his hands trembled, aching to skim over her body, to shape those round breasts, to taste her—he swallowed roughly and shook his head.

The previous night, while her shower ran, Michael had cleaned away the dishes and leashed himself from stepping into the steamy room. Instead, he'd turned on the television and Kylie had padded out into the living room, a towel wrapped around her head. Over her blue flannel pajamas, she wore a pink chenille robe and white socks covered her feet. With damp ringlets escaping the towel on her head, she had looked deliciously fresh and sweet and sexy. The soap and flowers scent she brought into the room had delicately curled around him. Michael's senses had reacted immediately when she'd yawned and stretched. He had forced his eyes away from the thrust of her unbound breasts beneath the heavy fabric. Due to the odd tightening in his throat, his words had been uneven and hoarse. "Go on up to bed, Kylie."

He shook his head again. The image of Kylie, scrubbed and soft and ready for bed had circled him all night. He didn't want to think of her in lace or nothing—creamy freckled silky skin, all those curves a man could lock onto and—

"Michael!" The feminine object of his thoughts peered around the stack of boxes, her hair tied up in a ribbon as blue as her eyes. "I've got a free hour. You haven't had that massage yet and you haven't seen what I've done since you did the wiring in the rough layout. How about stepping into my parlor?''

Michael's hands tightened on the wire he'd been splicing; his body tensed. He wasn't certain he liked how his body jerked to attention when Kylie was near. He'd always been in control, even in lovemaking, and he sensed that if Kylie touched him— ''Maybe some other time.''

''Okay, I'll call one of the guys. They've asked me to fit them in and now I've got a free hour. Michael, at this rate, I think I can manage to pay for a second massage bench.''

''Fit one of the guys into your schedule?'' Michael asked very carefully, thinking of where he'd like to fit into Kylie's life. ''I'll be right there.''

Kylie held the door open to the small room. Michael moved into it warily. He'd had sports massages for strained muscles, the worst in a bout with a five-hundred-pound wife abuser. The scents of oranges and roses curled around him, a burning candle lighting the shadows. A large, sheet covered bench dominated the cubicle. Little touches of Kylie and Anna—bundles of dried lavender, two of Gwyneth's small pots were filled with dried rose petal and orange peel potpourri. The small space seemed femininely soft when compared to the gym's men's massage areas. Michael was too aware of the intimacy within the room, of how close he would be to Kylie—without his clothes. The thought took his body lurching painfully and he breathed slowly, regaining control. Light, gentle flute music wafted in the room as Kylie spoke in her cool, even-toned professional voice, ''Remove your clothes, as many as you feel comfortable doing. Lie on your back and cover yourself with the sheets. Relax. Think pleasant thoughts. I'll be back in a minute.''

Michael undressed slowly. He wasn't certain about himself—how he would react to Kylie's hands upon his body, her nearness, that sweet feminine scent. The small bottle of oil sitting on a shelf jolted Michael. He suspected that she would be using that—she'd said on the mountain that she was without her oils and aromatherapy essentials. The oils were for— Michael swallowed tightly. Kylie would use the oil on his body—touching him. Nettled slightly because Kylie didn't seem affected by the knowledge that she would be touching his body, Michael eased down onto the bench. He tensed when he noted that the soft sheets had been warmed. The gentle rap at the door signaled Kylie. "Ready? Michael, I'll come back when you're lying on your back, okay?"

"This is fine." Michael turned to look at Kylie over his shoulder. His body tightened sensually. She was dressed in a long-sleeved sweater, sweatpants, earth sandals, and wearing her curls in that silky froth on top of her head. She looked sweet and sexy and round and firm and very warm. "Be gentle."

"You have to cooperate and relax. But until you have confidence in me—" She began gently massaging his scalp, finding his energy, and Michael felt himself drifting, giving himself to her fingers.

The sliding of the sheet down and upward until it only draped across his hips startled Michael. He held very still as the warm application of oil on Kylie's hands zapped him. She gently stroked down one side of his body and began on the other.

A half hour later, Kylie noted, "Hmm, how unusual. I can usually make most people melt in a half hour. You're gripping the sides of the bench and are more tense than when you came in. What's bothering you, Michael?"

"You," he said roughly, too aware of the steaming pressures of his body. He reached to grasp her wrist, preventing her from kneading his calf. "Don't touch me again."

She allowed him to draw her along the bench until she stood beside his head. She attempted to tug her wrist away and his hand only held her tighter. The stark contrast of that big male hand on her fragile wrist caused her to shiver. "You're touching me, Michael. That isn't how this works."

"Forget the massage, Kylie. You're tired. Is that what he did, work you until you dropped?"

Kylie closed her eyes against Michael's harsh expression. "Let's keep this on a professional basis, shall we? You found out all my problems that first night."

"Right now, I've got a few of my own."

"Like what?" she asked the heartbeat before he lithely pushed himself upright, still holding her wrist, and tugged her to stand between his knees.

"Like this." Michael's mouth descended upon hers and, before she could draw back, her body was answering the call of his hunger, her arms shot around his shoulders, her fingers digging in. She'd never been kissed so totally, and she opened herself to the taste, the excitement dancing on her lips, the hard feel— Michael's hands lowered, skimming her body warmly and then reached her bottom. In the next instant, she was lifted, straddling him.

"Michael…" She floated as he nibbled on her lips, tempting her, then she captured him, framed his hard jaw with her hands and held him still for her mouth.

"Say it again…my name, like that," Michael whispered as Kylie's hands skimmed his shoulders and smoothed his chest. The slightly rough texture intrigued her, the hard muscles wrapped tightly around her simmering with heat, setting off her body.

"We're going to fall off this bench," she managed to say unevenly.

Against her throat, his chuckle was rich and full and Kylie treasured the unfamiliar sound. "You're not so bad, Michael."

His parted lips slowly cruised up to her ear, his breath pounding through her like a tropical heat storm. Holding her with one arm, Michael drew up one of her feet, eased off the earth sandal and slid away her sock. His fingers began massaging gently, working each individual toe and her arch, his light kisses brushing across her lips. "You're very warm, dear heart."

"This candle is producing too much heat."

He chuckled again, the sound vibrating against her throat. "You're very…uh…flexible, Kylie."

"Yoga," she explained, then gave herself to the floating sensation. She sighed, leaning her head upon his shoulder. When Michael released her hair, easing it around her shoulders, she sighed again. "You studied this, didn't you?"

"Mmm. I'm learning."

"Thanks. I'll need to be more on top of it to deal with Leon and Sharon when they arrive— Uh!"

Michael placed her on her feet. He tossed her shoes and socks to her and crossed his arms over his chest, scowling at her. "What's this about your ex-husband?"

"He's going to work for me. He's very good at technique—"

"Work for you?" Michael repeated as if he thought the idea had leaped upon her from outer space. "*Your ex-husband?*"

"He could do better, but he just can't find a job that suits him. I can't pay very much, but until he gets some responsibility skills, I'd never forgive myself if anything happened to the baby. If it isn't diet food or instant, Sharon doesn't know anything about nutrition. I could work with her on that. For his part, Leon needs time to adjust to his new role as provider. Maybe I took some of that away from him. He's capable, I do know that. He just needs to rearrange his priorities, and if there is a place to do that it is here, in Freedom Valley. He could get new insights from the men here. That baby needs to be safe, Michael, and well nourished. It's just that they are in a spot right now and I can help. There's plenty of room at mom's house and she's been eating right and getting plenty of rest—''

''No,'' Michael said quietly, firmly.

She eyed him. ''I'm going to help them. My mother never turned away anyone in need, and neither will I. Especially when one of them is an unborn baby.''

''I should have known.'' Michael ran his hand through his hair, looking at her warily.

''I can use the extra help right now. Business is great.'' She wasn't certain of him now, as he studied her.

''Oh, I think it's all just great. Everything will work out, right? Leon will grow up, Sharon can learn how to be a mother, and you'll know that the baby will come into a better world, right?''

''Something like that.''

''Well, then, I'd like to help. I'd really like to help. They can stay at my place. Temporarily.''

''You're kidding!'' Karolina exclaimed in disbelief that night. She turned to Kylie, sitting next to her on the bed in Anna's upstairs room. ''Michael said it was okay for your ex-husband and his pregnant new wife to stay at his house?''

''They could have stayed here.'' The room was just as she had left it at nineteen. The quilt on her single bed had been made by her mother, a feminine blend of pale blues

and pinks and creams. Pictures of her in high school as a
cheerleader and as a graduate, ran across the antique dresser
that her father had refinished for her. Kylie wiggled her
toes, mourned the lack of a good reflexology treatment and
a pedicure, and studied the rug her mother had braided from
discarded clothing. She inhaled the fragrance of the dried
herbs and lavender that Gwyneth had thoughtfully placed
in the old glass vase. The hope chest her father had made
her when she was young stood against one wall, an array
of worn and beloved dolls propped over it. She'd filled it
with embroidery, because she and Miranda wanted to
please their mother. "I can't bear to open my hope chest.
It's like a step back into time. I'm a different person than
I was then."

"Mmm. Don't hand me that. More curves, just as caring
and sweet."

The springs on Kylie's single bed creaked as Karolina
raised her legs to the bed and crossed them. "Mmm. Mo-
tives. Why would Michael offer his house to your ex? No
one has ever been in it, but his women and your mother.
All of a sudden, it's open house time? The pieces don't fit.
Why?"

"I simply explained to him that I was getting more business than I could handle, and eventually I hoped to take on
help. Leon and Sharon are in financial straits now and with
the baby coming...basically, Leon called and he needs
work. He's willing to take lower wages in return for a place
to stay."

"Where will Michael stay?"

"I suppose he'll stay in his house. It's just a temporary
thing, but Michael was adamant once I told him that they
might be staying here for a while. He didn't think the stairs
would be good for Sharon, since she's pregnant, and he has
a single level home. I thought his offer was very generous."

"I'll bet." Karolina's eyes narrowed on her friend. "He doesn't want you around Leon, that's why. I warned him off you after that kiss at the Silver Dollar, but I can see I'll have to step in and—uh! You just hit me with a pillow! Bet you meals for a week that you can't get into Michael's house—uh!"

"Why would I want to? Uh!" Kylie grabbed the pillow that had just hit her.

"Bet he keeps files and has a hidden wall layered with weapons. He's probably got shrunken heads and spears and bombs and I'd kill to get his black book. I'll bet it's got numbers in it that you wouldn't find anywhere." The phone interrupted her suspicions. She waited while Kylie answered the ringing telephone. Due at a mandatory library board meeting, Karolina let herself out while Kylie talked quietly with Miranda.

Kylie lay in the shadows of the room for a long time after ending the call with her sister. Miranda wasn't releasing her problems and that meant they were deep and private and she was trying to work them out. Kylie's meticulous, organized older sister missed their mother and Freedom Valley, but she wasn't ready to come back...not just yet.

On impulse, Kylie retrieved a favorite rag doll from the top of the hope chest and cuddled it to her. She couldn't bear to read her mother's journals, the ones Tanner had carefully placed amid the pictures of their relatives on Anna's cherished buffet. There were pages missing, Tanner had said, but they were meant for him and Gwyneth alone. He hoped that Kylie and Miranda would find what he had, the healing of home.

Kylie hugged the doll tighter, and used one tiny stuffed

arm to dry her tears. "Mom? I can't bear to read them. I can't bear to open this chest."

Shh. Go to sleep. Everything will be just fine. Was that the sound of her mother's voice? Or was it the sound of wind hurling dried leaves against the windowpanes?

Six

If it's a good match of the heart, the woman is hunting as much as he, or more. She'll have her dreams and she'll have her love, settling for nothing less.
—Anna Bennett's Journal

Leon and Sharon arrived on the first day of November. At eleven o'clock that night Michael lay on his sleeping bag. Filled with down, it spread across the narrow cot in the rear of his 1880s building. The two-story former Freedom Valley Mercantile Goods building creaked around him, scents from Kylie's oils as disturbing as his thoughts. A civilized dinner at his house as Kylie made Leon and Sharon welcome had been frustrating. Leon was blond and calendar-model perfect...and shallow and spoiled and vain. At eight months into her pregnancy, Sharon, a frothy mass of bleached hair and smoothly tanned, muscle-honed body, had mourned her not-so-flat stomach and relaxing pelvic

girdle. She had picked at the wholesome tuna casserole
Kylie had prepared while changing sheets and unpacking
the couple's clothing and washing and drying them. Some-
time between all that, Kylie had met her appointment at
Soft Touches with the coach of the football team—forty-
year-old Don Rayburn wasn't a match for the high school
boys, but he had tried and now ached in every muscle.

While once Michael could have been distracted by his
growing financial accounts, his desperation to succeed, he
settled deeper into his dark, brooding thoughts. More comfortable alone and in the shadows, he forced himself to
relax for the first time all evening. The insight into Kylie's
married life hadn't been pleasant. Leon and Sharon were
thoughtless and incapable of funding their lives, and they
left an untidy trail behind them as they settled into Michael's guest bedroom. Fearing that he would say too much,
Michael had helped Kylie clear away the dishes. She had
been too quiet and pale, and he knew how much she'd
wanted the baby that Sharon now carried.

Furious and frustrated, Michael had gone to the Silver
Dollar to mull the situation in the shadows with a draft
beer. He needed the foamy suds as a special treat to himself
while he brooded about Kylie. Toting giant sacks of ham-
burgers, fries and cola, the Bachelor Club had dropped over
later to his shop to play poker. It was then that he received
his issue of The Rules for Bride Courting.

Earlier that day, Fidelity Moore had stopped Dakota
Jones and asked him to play messenger, transporting a ribbon wrapped copy of The Rules for Bride Courting to Michael. Fidelity's choice of Dakota left little room for
doubt—Dakota was known to be woman-shopping for a
mother to the child he wanted. Since Michael was to be the
recipient of the 1880s manual on the conduct of a man

seeking a bride, Fidelity had chosen Kylie's suitor and potential bridegroom.

Michael snorted and stared at the book, propped up on his workbench and mocking him. He couldn't see Kylie choosing him for the last dance of the Women's Council's quarterly socials—that forthright claiming of him would demonstrate to all of Freedom Valley that she'd chosen him to be her husband. Michael rubbed his forehead, an unfamiliar headache brewing as he rehashed the day and the people moving through it.

Kylie had described her ex-husband's reasons for coming to Freedom to Willa, the mayor and the owner of the Wagon Wheel Café. Willa, in turn, had served coffee, pie and various lower-than-a-snake's-belly versions of Kylie's ex-husband. Dakota Jones and York Meadows planned to be extra friendly with Leon, inviting him to participate in the local rodeo. An introduction to Little Twister was planned—Leon just might enjoy the two-thousand pound bucking bull. Dylan Spotted Horse was disgusted by a man who bleached his hair, applied baby oil to his muscles and strutted across a stage in a "rig" that barely covered the essentials. On the other hand, Dylan thought massaging women for a livelihood would be "mighty fine."

Michael glanced at the lights of the alarm system he had activated at his house. They remained constant and silent; his office door remained locked. Late night alerts from Rosa would be delivered on his pager and he would return her call.

Michael needed time to think about Kylie and her emotions. He preferred not to think about that first night, and her admitted lack of sex and simmering needs. While the dark ways of life had not touched Kylie, his innocence had been shattered in childhood. He'd seen the good and right dreams women should have twisted and torn into ugliness.

Used to dealing with business and not his emotions, Michael had tried to concentrate on the files now discarded beside his cot. It was his job as a silent partner to research potential troublesome clients applying for security. He usually enjoyed searching for minute details, background checks and weighing pitfalls of difficult cases, but Kylie and his emotions prevented clinical dissection of the facts. From a destitute background, Michael had been meticulous about his personal finances. When they'd asked him to do so, he usually enjoyed checking on the women's accounts, making suggestions to help them rebuild their lives and financial security. Now, not even his investment portfolio held his attention.

At the moment, his own needs seemed to be in overdrive, outweighing his logical decision to protect Kylie from the storms inside him, the need to sink into her, to take, to make her essence a part of his. He'd tried to settle down for an all-night session with his electronic notebook, working on a new security system suitable for women's shelters and halfway houses. One wrong move, one brush of his body against hers, those soft breasts…. Michael realized that his forehead was damp with sweat, his body aching. Tomorrow morning, he'd leave early, maybe up to the mountains for fishing and concentrating on getting his life back under control.

He frowned as metal crashed outside the back steps; Freedom Valley had few prowlers. Corralled to the back of the building in an area once used for drovers' horses, Jack nickered. A key rattled in the old door lock, the brass knob turning slowly. Michael watched the rotating metallic gleam in the shadows. He hadn't installed a security system in the old building, preferring to keep the antique hardware and original condition. The door opened a crack, outlining the small, compact intruder. He wore a bulky jacket, a knit cap covering his head.

Michael had warned twelve-year-old Johnny Johnson about his mischief. The boy reminded him of himself at that age, except Johnny's parents loved him too much, spoiling him, excusing his minor offenses. This time, Johnny would have something to remember.

Michael lay very still as the door closed quietly and the small intruder moved cautiously toward him in the shadows. The intruder's legs bumped Michael's cot and Kylie cried softly, "Oh, Michael. What happened? You must have heard me come in. Are you hurt? Why haven't you said something?"

Stunned by the identity of the intruder, Michael lay still, trying to focus on Kylie's face above him. For a moment, he thought he was asleep and dreaming. Then Kylie grabbed his flannel shirt, catching an amount of chest hair with it, and shook him. The taut hairs on his chest painfully reminded him that he wasn't sleeping as Kylie's urgent voice quivered in the shadows. "Wake up! Wake up! No. Stay here. I'll get help. Oh, I'll never forgive myself if something has happened to you."

He realized that the hand he had raised to protect himself from the intruder had formed possessively around layers of clothing and a round, soft breast. "I'm fine," he whispered unevenly, overcome by her uniquely natural feminine scent.

Dear heart. She was his other half, filling his heart with warmth and his body with the need to hold her close and dear. She was the softness he'd searched for all his life, his completion, his sunshine in the shadows. He moved his hand cautiously, easing aside her jacket to caress Kylie's breast. "Why are you here?"

"Why are you lying down? Why are you here? Why

aren't you at your house?'' she returned in a hushed whisper.

Instantly the air between them seemed to be charged with tiny lightning bolts that skittered around his body, hardening it. ''I want you,'' he said baldly, because he wanted to leave no doubt in Kylie's mind about his intentions. ''I don't want to complain about you grabbing me, because it's a compliment that you want me, too. But I'd appreciate it if you'd let go of my shirt. There's a fair amount of hair being pulled by your fists.''

''Oh. Sorry,'' Kylie whispered, releasing him. Reluctantly, Michael forced his hand away from her breast and sat up. It disgusted him that with Kylie, he'd made good his youthful nickname of ''Fast Hands Cusack.'' Her eyes were wide and silver upon him, her face too pale as he stood to rip away the knitted cap covering the hair he loved to touch, to hold, to smell.

''Why are you here?'' she asked quietly as he hurled the cap away, not bothering to conceal his ill temper. ''I stopped by your house to check on Leon and Sharon and you weren't there. Karolina said you were having a beerfest at the tavern, dancing close with Fredricka, and playing poker all night with the Bachelor Club. Karolina suspects there is an orgy brewing. You wouldn't have any part of an orgy, would you, Michael?'' Kylie asked shakily, as if she couldn't bear the thought.

Michael knew his body, and it wanted slow, satisfying lovemaking with one woman—Kylie. But he wanted promises and tenderness and tomorrows, too. At the moment, he didn't trust himself with her. He detested his unpredictable, emotional, vulnerable state.

''An orgy. Super Snoop's expectations are high.'' He'd seen Karolina peeking around the corner of the women's rest room at the tavern. Because Chuck Berry's rock and roll guitar was vibrating sound loud enough to be heard on the moon, Michael had leaned close to listen to Fredricka's greenhouse electrical problems. She wanted a new strain of tulip bulbs to sprout faster for display and marketing purposes and correct lighting was essential. Statuesque Fredricka might have been curved and luscious and athletic, but it was Kylie who fitted into Michael's arms and his heart. He rubbed his hand roughly on his jeans, but the warm softness of her breast remained to haunt him.

"I wanted to apologize for everything, for making you uncomfortable in your own home."

Michael continued to study her. He didn't want to think about trying to sleep in his own bed hours earlier, but Leon's guttural sounds and rocketing, "Yes…yes…yes!" had preceded a shout of male release. To think of Kylie's body with Leon made Michael want to tear the boards from the wall, the adobe bricks from the building, the heart from Leon's pretty bodybuilder body. "So he and you were Yin and Yang, were you? Each complementing and supporting the other, fulfilling each other?"

"Not exactly," Kylie answered, and studied the shadows of the room, avoiding looking at him. She flushed in the shadows. "This place has got so much history. Cattle drovers used to stop here for supplies and research potential brides…Leon and Sharon were quite busy when I stopped in—um…exercising, I think—but Leon asked me for the loan of my pickup."

"You didn't—"

"They're penniless with a baby coming, Michael. I borrowed your mountain bike and rode into town. I needed the exercise. It was a beautiful ride— Stop muttering and scowling. You're coming home with me. I feel too bad to leave you here when you should be in your own bed. You can ride Jack. No, you're not staying out at the Boat House, the new building Tanner built for his business. You're going to be comfortable. We can work on your intimacy and relationship skills. We'll watch football games and romantic old movies together. I won't tell anyone if you drop a tear or two."

"You heard me say I wanted you, didn't you?" Michael asked unsteadily.

"Yes, of course I did. It's obvious there is something humming between us by the way my heart starts to flutter at the sight of you and I get all warm and melty inside. But it's also obvious that my sexual generators are highly charged and you're an experienced man who knows women. But we can manage a few days at Mom's until Leon and Sharon find a place of their own. I'm going to borrow money to help them rent a house and—"

Michael's momentary cherished hope that Kylie could be seeing him as her Yang, her masculine half, her completion, slid into a cold dangerous pit. "Oh, no, you're not. And they're not staying with us, either. This isn't a foursome and he's not watching you do those yoga exercises."

Kylie's eyes flashed in the shadows, her mouth firmed. "I don't need his advice. There is nothing wrong with my yoga technique. It's wonderful for centering."

"He's a man, isn't he?" Michael demanded, resenting the Kylie-crack in his control. He blinked as the thought of watching Kylie center within herself smacked him. She'd be beautiful, serene, and her center would be— He realized his voice sounded strangled when he repeated, "'Centering.'"

Michael scrubbed his hands roughly over his face. He had no right to think of Kylie's perfectly focused center.

"He never noticed when I did yoga exercises in the nine years we were married. He liked to watch his own muscles too much. But then most of that time we were in separate bedrooms. He didn't like sharing his bed—until Sharon, and that's understandable. She's very appealing and pretty…. You're not telling me what to do, are you, Michael?'' Kylie challenged softly, dangerously.

''You're saying you don't think you're appealing?'' Michael was disgusted by his tone of obvious outrage, his frustration that another man would not find Kylie as feminine and sweet and lusty and hot and earthy as he did.

He flipped over that thought. He didn't want another man to be as fascinated with Kylie as he was. He wasn't certain that he liked the power she had to upset him. Fragile wasn't his safe and confident zone.

Michael strained for control. For him, marriage to Kylie would mean her in his bed, in his arms, him filling her every night, pledging lives and hearts and— He raked his fingers through his hair. ''You're damned appealing. Perfectly appealing. Always have been. Exciting, provocative, intelligent. There isn't another woman like you on earth. You're sexy and smart and talented, to say nothing of great curves—great breasts and hips—and a great mind and a loving heart. I love to hear you laugh, all low and soft, and the way your eyes sparkle and dance… And the graceful way you move—like an earth goddess on the prowl, ready to mate, like fluid, molten… It's enough to make a man want to carry you off— Now don't you think all that would make a man take notice?''

Michael closed his lips. His outburst had shattered him. He should have presented his thoughts in a better arrangement, and not laced with the elemental sensual desire rocketing through his veins and lodging hot and hard in his body. Kylie should have smooth, romantic words, logically placed to make her feel attractive.

Kylie spoke breathlessly. ''Wow. You see me like that? Even on a bad hair day?''

He thought about how he wanted to bury his face in Kylie's silky soft curls, how he wanted it to flow over his body as they made love, giving to one another. He pushed those words back into his heart and was grateful for the shadows covering his embarrassed flush. How could he explain how he felt when he was with her, like the world was new and good and would go on forever? How could he tell her how silky her skin ran beneath his fingers? How could he tell her how he might feel if his child were nestling in her body and dreams really did come true? A woman should have romantic words to please her, and Michael's were stored tightly in his heart, glowing there like sunshine. She was his first love and she frightened him—his emotions frightened him. Fear wasn't an emotion that sat easily upon Michael Cusack, tough lone-wolf guy. "You're okay," he murmured finally.

Kylie watched him with interest, her eyes silvery in the night. She licked her lips and the sensual jolt slammed into Michael's body. The seductive feminine waves she emitted now were enveloping and tugging him erotically as she whispered, "I don't think there is anything more exciting than you right now, right here. You seem all quivery, as though your antennae are shifting and sparking like a lightning rod on a barn just waiting for a big bolt to hit. You look as if one touch would set you off."

"Maybe. From you, just maybe. I'm beginning to doubt my past experiences with zapping. You present a new concept of the word. Let us not talk about rods and big bolts. I'd like to hear more about your overcharged generators and how you get all melty inside. I've got some concept— working with electricity as I do—how electric jolts can zap and melt. But I can't come home with you tonight, sweetheart," Michael stated darkly. "And this is why."

Kylie met Michael's hot open mouth with her own, grabbing his shoulders to keep him anchored to her, her fingers digging into all the fine, hard muscle. His body flexed as he tore off his shirt and undershirt, tossing them away as the kiss deepened, slanted, tongues enticing, suckling.

She'd never been held like this, desired like this—with hunger and yet with tenderness. She'd never wanted like this. "Michael…" she heard herself sigh over the pounding beat of her blood.

The dancing of her heart, the center of her body heating, quivering, all seemed just the right symphony with Michael's taste, promising a gift she'd always wanted. She nibbled on his lips, frantically keeping him close as he eased away her jacket.

The rough intake of his breath was just what she wanted to hear as he swept away her sweatshirt to leave her unbound breasts exposed to his gaze. His hands trembled as they slowly moved to cover her, cupping her. "You're beautiful," he whispered. "Perfect."

When his head lowered, his lips pressing against the softness, Kylie cried out, holding him tight against her. His open mouth suckled gently, tightening the heated cords running throughout her body, weakening her knees. The textures of his rough skin, the lick of his tongue, the gentle pressure of his teeth tore through her.

"Hold me, Michael," she whispered against his hair. "Hold me hard against you."

He gently treated her other breast before straightening and easing her body against his. The cords and muscles of his body melded hotly against her softer one, and the sensation was perfect as Michael's caresses lowered to her bottom. Then he tugged the knot at her sweatpants waistband, loosening it and her pants fell to her ankles, leaving her body without the shield of underclothing.

Michael's hands cupped her bottom instantly, fingers

slightly squeezing, and his voice was raw and uneven against her throat. He stared blankly at her bare stomach, the juncture at her thighs and his breath seemed to shatter even as it hit the air between them. "Kylie. Kylie? Aren't you missing something?"

Everything was right in place and aching. "Laundry," she explained hurriedly, not wanting to break his lovely concentration, his hunger. "I was doing laundry before going to your house, so I took them off and dropped them in the washer. I've been working so hard that I'm behind in housework."

He breathed unevenly, his hands cupping her bottom tightly. His violent pulse rocketed against her lips as he trembled. He muttered something as though he were helpless. Then he sighed roughly as if giving up the battle and one hand slid to press against her stomach. His touch lowered to cup her, gently invading and Kylie held very still adjusting to the unique smoothing of his fingers. He supported her weight, giving her pleasure— "Michael?"

"Kylie. No. You should have—"

"You. I want you. Now." She found the snap of his jeans and unable to open them, she cried out, "Help me, Michael."

Over the layer of denim, her hand found him and Michael held very still. Then one touch of his hand sent her reeling, rocketing, tightening... She took the sensations into her, hoarding them, feasting upon the exquisite pleasure and letting it burn her without restraint until the fire gently died and she leaned against him, drained and floating and wonderful. She snuggled to Michael, her safe port in the storm, kissing his chest, inhaling his fragrance, smoothing his trembling body to keep him warm and close.

"Kylie?" Michael whispered against her ear.

"Don't move. Don't breathe. Just hold me," she returned, holding her pleasure close and tight inside.

"I'm taking you home." Michael's tone held amusement and as he eased her away from him, his hands trembled. His sweeping hot stare down her body pleased her.

Then, unused to the prolonged intensity, Kylie crossed her arm over her sensitive breasts. She lowered her other hand to conceal her femininity. "It's rude to stare," she whispered, her throat drying.

His eyes tore through the shadows, burning an upward path to hers, raising a prickling heat upon her skin. She breathed unevenly, willing him to come to her, to take what she had to offer. Unsteady, Michael said firmly, "That's why I can't go home with you."

She'd just offered her heart and her body and her home, and he was tossing logic into the magic between them, tearing it apart.

"You don't think I can manage this? That I don't have control over my own—body?" She bent to jerk up her sweatpants and when her shaking hands failed to tie the waistband knot, Michael took over the task.

Holding her hand, he bent slowly to retrieve her sweatshirt. He stuffed her arms into it, and tugged it over her head as if she were a child. "I can almost hear you thinking, Michael," Kylie whispered as he eased her arms into the sleeves of her jacket and zipped it closed as she would her heart. Her marriage to one man had been a lie. She'd given herself—all of herself too easily—not leaving enough to preserve her pride. With Michael, she intended to have honesty and her due as a woman.

"What am I thinking?" His tone was detached, cool, guarded, his expression hardening.

She watched him draw on his shirt. "That I'm Anna's daughter, and Tanner and Miranda's sister. That you're going to try to take care of me. I won't have you on those terms. I want what runs true between us. I want magic and my dreams.''

"Mmm," he murmured without confirming her statement. "What makes you think I can give you those?''

"You just can and you know it. You're too mulish to admit that you have dreams, too.''

"Dreams are for the innocent. I'm not.''

He was retreating into his shields again, all that lovely heat and emotion slipping away. Kylie followed her instincts to keep him close and placed her hands on his cheeks. She spoke from her heart, out of desperation to keep him from his shadows. "I can't bear to think of you here…that you're here because of me. Come home with me, Michael. You can sleep in Tanner's old room. It's just a temporary situation.''

"'A temporary situation,'" he repeated thoughtfully. He smiled softly, and toyed with her hair, arranging it on her shoulders. "Across the hall from yours?''

"I'll protect you from gossip, Michael. *You have to come home with me now.*" She had to claim him for her own, to keep him close.

"Are you saying you want to adopt me because I'm temporarily a man without a home, an orphan? Or are you saying you want to be with me?''

He'd torn apart her magic a moment ago, and this time she guarded her heart, giving him little to destroy. She'd have him on her terms, in good time. "Does it matter?''

From lips that had been soft and hungry against her skin and demanding, Michael's words were harsh. "Call it.''

She didn't want to be pushed, not after such heaven. "Be reasonable.''

"I'm feeling plenty—and none of it is reasonable, sweetheart.''

She searched his scowl, that muscle running taut and furious along his jaw. "It's that 'man' thing, isn't it? Oh, I wish I understood better."

"It's simple. I want to know where I stand."

"Well, it isn't sympathy, I can tell you that. You don't deserve sympathy," she tossed back hotly at him. "But I've got my pride, too, you know. I've caused you an inconvenience and I want to make it up. Neighbors do that here in Freedom Valley."

"Is that all?" His words were dark and cutting in the night.

"No," she answered truthfully. She followed her need to place herself in his care, to lean softly against him, to nestle her face against his warm throat. "There's more."

Michael tilted her face up to his. "Show me."

The demand was soft, yet age old and she met his lips with truth and hunger. There was just that satisfying tensing of Michael's body before he took her mouth with a passionate certainty that couldn't be misunderstood.

On the ride home, seated upon Jack, Michael behind her, he slid his hand beneath her coat. He held her close and tight against him. He caressed her gently bobbing breasts as if touching her gave him pleasure and ease. She felt erotic, seductive, desired and at peace with being a woman who a man liked to touch. Then, when she'd turned to capture his wonderful mouth, to breathe that dark scent upon his skin, his touch had lowered to gently pleasure her again. Warm and limp, she slid from the saddle into his arms and he carried her into the house. At the foot of the stairs leading to her bedroom, he put her firmly away from him. "Good night, Kylie. Go to bed. I'll unsaddle Jack and be in later."

She'd had that much, those callused but tender hands giving her back a part of the magic she'd found earlier. She treasured the taste of his mouth, the hard pounding of his heart, the desperate hunger for her leashed, and she vowed to tear it from him, to make it her own.

From her upstairs window, the lace curtain drawn aside, she watched him. Outlined in the moonlight, he'd been too alone, the cold wind whipping at him. She'd wanted to run to him, to give him her heart and hold him safe, but she knew he wouldn't appreciate comfort now, not while he was fighting himself. She stood at the top of the stairs and waited, listening to him move through her mother's house—the closing of a door, water running in the downstairs shower. It didn't surprise her, as she waited, to hear him open her mother's kitchen cabinet, and glass clinked as he poured bourbon kept to ease dark storms. Kylie knew then that Michael had likely visited her mother, and had been offered more than blackberry wine for comfort.

Kylie looked down at the man, dressed only in his jeans, at the bottom of the stairs. In the shadows, Michael met her gaze. The air shifted and tingled and prickled; with each breath her nipples dragged upon the rough inner texture of her sweatshirt reminding her of his caress, the need rocketing through them both. "Good night, Michael," she whispered unevenly, glad for the sight of him standing there, when he could have ridden away. "You'll be coming up to bed soon then."

"I will."

"I'll have my dreams," she said finally, to set him straight and leave no room for doubt between them. *And I'll have you, my love,* she thought as she closed her bedroom door. She listened to the boards creak under his weight as he passed and prayed that in time he would learn to trust her with his heart.

Seven

Not all men know who they are, in their hearts, until love changes them.
—Anna Bennett's Journal

Kylie awoke to the sound of birds chattering outside her window. Sunlight streamed through the lace curtains, and pleasured by the warm bloom within her, she stretched in her bed. She ran her fingertips across the fine delicate stitches of her quilt, and wiggled her toes against the daffodil splashed sheets. For the first time in years, her body was totally relaxed, her mind not leaping ahead into her day, planning what to do and how much time to allow for the task. Habit made her glance at the bedside clock she had turned facedown upon returning to Freedom Valley—she'd been conditioned to run on a minute-by-minute treadmill and she'd wanted freedom to think.

She placed her hand over her heart, and the heavy thump

told her that she wasn't dreaming. Out of habit, and still half asleep, she yawned and stretched and padded to the upstairs shower, taking her time to shampoo and wallow in the jojoba and chamomile oil she had added to ordinary liquid soap. Just a drop of ylang ylang added sensuality, and today, she was definitely feeling like a woman. She hummed, the sound echoing her sense of well-being. Once again, she was in control of her life, harmony pouring through her like honey. *She was powerful and feminine and—*

In her bedroom, Kylie studied the woman in the oval mirror and ran a fingertip across her lips, her body humming with the need to dive into Michael's bed and feast upon him. But oh, no, she'd let him sleep and awake to a proper breakfast. He needed tending and time to adjust to being with her. She'd make the transition easy for him and instead of leaping into his bed, she'd wait—

The clatter of horses' hooves echoed from her mother's driveway. Kylie went to the window. For a moment she stood still, her warm floating well-being mood ripped away. Tanner and Michael rode in the lead, and behind them were Koby, Gabriel, York, Fletcher and all the rest. Michael's head turned just then. Through the sunlight and the distance to her upstairs bedroom, his stare was as hard and grim as if he'd never touched her, never breathed unevenly against her skin, never held her as the tropical wind and heat swept through her.

He couldn't do that—he couldn't ignore what had just happened between them. He couldn't ignore the storms between them, the way their souls seemed to touch. Kylie jerked open the window and yelled, "Michael! Stop!"

The cold morning air hit her body, and she realized that nothing covered her but her comfortable old flannel robe.

She jerked it together and called again, "Where are you going?"

"Town," Tanner returned, but Michael continued to stare at her. Fear lurched through her, chilling her; his expression offered no warmth or future or dreams.

I'll have my dreams, she'd said. Michael still tasted her lips, too giving and warm, her body too yielding to his touch. She should have everything a woman in Freedom Valley would want of a man. His body was rigid with the need to ride back to her, to run up the stairs and carry her into town.

He'd stop gossip about Kylie by appearing before the Women's Council, an emergency meeting arranged by Fidelity. He wanted the right to protect her against her user of an ex-husband. He'd let them know how he felt, dragging the words from his soul to serve them to the Council, the task difficult for him. Michael sucked in the cold morning air and circled his need to provide Kylie with the old-fashioned standards set long ago. Tradition weighed heavily in Freedom Valley, and Kylie had a right to take her place. He couldn't bring himself to tell her that he was that old-fashioned, that romance prowled his heart when he thought of her. *If he were to make a fool of himself, he'd prefer to do it without the woman he loved watching him.*

Unused to the emotions and moving too quickly without planning, Michael looked away from Kylie. He'd find a way to tell her, but not now, not with the need prowling through him to make his intentions known.

In traditionally based Freedom Valley, it was important for the man desiring a wife to make his heart known. However, to a man who lived privately, taking that step out of the shadows was difficult. Michael had shared little of his life with anyone and unused to sharing, he preferred to follow his instincts. He wanted nothing to interfere with his

plans to take that step, to face the women of the Council—
including Kylie.

Foolish fear? Maybe. But this morning, he was out to set
claim to his woman and his future. He was taking "The
Leap." Anything could set her off, challenging him, some
minor point would cause an argument, and then the whole
big beautiful morning dream would be shot to hell.

He wasn't in a mood to have his dreams dissected or
delayed. Every instinct in him told him this was right and
logical, for a man to set claim to the woman he loved.

The morning was right. The woman was right. He'd find
a way to tell her later, he thought, even as the word "cow-
ard" came slipping through him. He snorted in disgust at
the word, and images of brawls and dangerous situations
cut at him. Yet this one woman could make him tremble.
A man had a right to romance on the morning he was
publicly making known his intentions.

Michael scowled at Tanner, who was watching him.
"She gets to me," Michael said roughly and ignored the
men's laughter. "If I tell her what I'm doing, she'll start a
ruckus and I'm not in the mood for that this morning. I'll
tell her later."

"You'll have to do better than that at the Women's
Council," her brother said, grinning. "But I know how it
is when a woman is in a snit and you've got romance on
your mind. She'll have your scalp if she finds out before
you tell her."

Michael snorted again. "I'll take my chances. I can't tell
how she'll react to anything. Let's just do this."

Kylie dressed hurriedly, tying on her running shoes. She
had to talk to Michael this morning, to know that Tanner
hadn't called him out. She couldn't have them fighting, not
her beloved brother and her—the man she wanted to take
as her lover—Michael was already her friend.

He'd left her without an explanation. He couldn't put up those walls again. Kylie sailed out of the house, jerking on her jacket as she ran. She took the path over the hill, the shortest route to Freedom. After a half-mile of realizing she was out of shape for distance running, and plotting how she would wrap her hands around his muscular neck and squeeze slowly, Kylie managed to call, "Michael!"

The other men's horses nickered and stamped nervously as she pushed her way through the bushes to look up at Tanner and Michael. Neither man welcomed her, Tanner's expression as cold and grim as Michael's. "I won't have you in this, Tanner," she said.

"Won't you?" His tone challenged her, gripped his right as her older brother to care for her.

"No." She studied Michael, searching for bruises that Tanner's angry fist might have made. Michael was freshly shaved, a nick just there on his cheek, and nothing about him was sweet and tender. This morning her razor had been damp and from the gleam on his cheeks and the tiny nicks, she knew he'd used it, probably snarling all the while. The sunlight struck his jutting cheekbone, skin gleaming upon the hard angle. Blue-black sparks danced on his hair, a glossy strand tossed by the slight cold breeze—or was that her heart freezing, accepting that he did not care enough to see her after last night? The cold morning air swept around her, lifted her hair away from her face. How could he touch her so beautifully and then ride away from her as if nothing had happened? "You're wearing Tanner's shirt. The one I gave him for his birthday and the tie I gave him for Christmas. Why?"

"My selection was limited this morning." He shrugged and a searching glance at Tanner told her nothing. She flushed under the weight of his inspection, his little sister who had just spent the night yet again with Michael Cusack. She lifted her head and met his gaze, for she would have only truth between her brother and herself. He gave her nothing, no reassurance that he approved, though he would know that she held his love and thoughts dear.

"Where are you going?" She searched Michael's face, the horses stamping around her, ready to be off. The steam from their nostrils shot into the chilly air as she searched the faces of the men she'd known all her life. They gave her nothing, the boys she had taunted and cherished and the men that she held dear as friends.

"To town," Michael said finally as if he resented giving her the tidbit.

"To do what? Why are you all riding today and so early?" She fought to keep the panic from her voice and her eyes, and Michael's gaze was too narrowed, green cutting at her, tearing at her heart.

She'll destroy me, Michael brooded. *She'll stop me from doing what's right, asking for her. I'll find a way to tell her later.*

"We've got business to keep," Tanner stated abruptly and Michael slid a grateful look at him.

"So early? And Michael wearing a tie? When has he ever worn a tie? It's one of yours. Why would he borrow your tie?" Terror twisted around her, choking her, as she searched Michael's face. He looked away from her, sitting very straight in the saddle. She read the dark flush in his cheeks, that anger tightening his beautiful mouth. He wasn't answering her, believing he owed her nothing.

Oh, there are rules and there are rules, she thought darkly, her anger growing by the heartbeat, welling over her. *You show me beauty, and then you deny doing so?*

Tanner was kinder, her brother who had always cared for her. "Go back to the house, Kylie. You're shivering."

The morning chill swept clear through her, ice tightening about her heart.

"I've got work to do…a schedule to keep…a business to run." *And pride to keep, Michael Cusack. I won't be running after you.* "Which one of you is giving me a ride?"

Michael seemed to tense, but then again, perhaps he felt nothing. He remained still and unmoved, his collar turned up at his throat, his eyes staring at the road leading into Freedom. How could he? How could he not remember—?

"Choose," Michael ordered curtly as the horses tramped around her. She placed her hand on Jack's cheek when he turned to nuzzle her, a kinder heart than the man who rode him.

Michael knew he was handling her too roughly, pushing her. But his pride demanded a small bit of satisfaction. He didn't have time to learn the softer ways to reach Kylie's gentle heart, but he would. Instincts as old as the world drove him now, to claim her in a ritual that had long been observed in Freedom Valley. He'd never love another woman, let her roam gently in his heart and it was time to let others know of his intentions.

There in the sunlight dancing through the naked limbs of the trees bordering the road, while the dead leaves rustled in the breeze, Kylie looked at the men she knew well. She looked at Tanner and because Michael had withdrawn behind his shields and because he had to pay, she tossed her words to the clear fresh air for all to know. "I choose you," she said to Michael, challenging him with her look. "I want to ride with you and torture you."

"You've done enough of that already." His words were dark and resentful, but there was a soft curl to his lips. The slight crinkling beside his meadow-green eyes said that he was enjoying her frustration.

*What were the rules dancing in the frosty air? What did
he want from her that she'd given, and that he'd counted
as a score on his side?* Dazzled by his widening grin, she
fought the thundering need to pull his head down and take
his mouth— *What had she given him?* "It's miles into
town. You know I don't have my pickup."

Dead upon the trees, the leaves rustled in the cold wind
that circled her and Michael. They seemed alone, despite
the stamping of the horses and the steam shooting from
their nostrils. Men she'd known all her life faded in com-
parison to this one man, a rugged scar running across his
cheek and danger flashing in his eyes. Kindness wasn't in
them as he pinned her on the earth beneath him, locked her
shoes and her heart with that steady unreadable expression.
Caught by the wind, his hair riffled and shifted and her
hand ached to smooth it again, to feel that bold texture
against her body as he asked, "Won't someone else do?
Can't you terrorize someone else for the distance?"

She didn't understand the hope and pride in his tone, not
the man she would destroy. He'd flung more to the wind
curling between them than the question of whose horse
she'd share— She didn't understand what he wanted from
her. "No. They're all sweethearts. You're the one who
isn't."

The warmth in his expression slid away into the frosty
air, stamped by the horses ready to be off. "You give too
much."

Her head went up at that verbal jab. She was no less than
he in this small war amid the cold wind and the waiting
men intent upon the battle. She let her hair swirl around
her, let the wind take it back from her face so that Michael
Cusack could read the truth in her heart. She wasn't one to
hide her emotions. "I give what I want."

"You chose me. You can change your mind now, if you want."

The odd formality wasn't like Michael, but his eyes were fierce and demanding upon her. The rules were shifting, tossed by the wind, emotions flying between them. She gripped the truth that ran strong within her. "I do choose you, Michael Cusack."

Tanner nodded briefly, making his own decisions as he watched the warring play between them. Michael's eyes narrowed into green slits, ripping down her body as if to terrify her, to make her change her mind. But backing off from a fight with him wasn't on her menu, not now when Michael slowly extended his hand. The hard warmth curled around her own. She slid her foot into the stirrup he had vacated and swung up behind him.

Time hadn't changed much, Kylie decided darkly as they rode through the sunlight. She was still the tagalong, the unwanted demanding her place among them. But now there was no teasing among the men, no groans or belches or threats to keep her away. Kylie held Michael tight, not wanting him to leave her. She leaned against his back, nuzzling it with her cheek. "You're up to no good, Michael Cusack."

He laughed then and reached behind him to smooth her back, keeping her close to him for a bit. It was a small thing, but reassuring and she settled for that, trusting him.

She flushed as they rode into town, the horses hooves clip-clopping, echoing violently in her heart. Leonard came out from his gas station, and JoAnn and Eli from the bakery. Eli placed his arm around his wife, and there were tears in JoAnn's eyes. In the Wagon Wheel, Willa stood amid the breakfast crowd gathered at the window. They'd be thinking of her mother and of her honor, and of how

Kylie had spent the night with Michael, who sat too straight, ignoring her as if he had never touched her.

"Let me off here." She slid from Jack's rump and still Michael didn't move, rigid and looking straight ahead. She could have killed him for not sparing her a look after last night's beautiful kisses. She hurried to unlock Soft Touches and turned to stare at the men watching her. Tenderness lingered in their hard expressions, but determination, too.

Michael hadn't noticed her, hadn't said a word to her all the five miles into town. Just one word could have saved the tearing of her heart, could have saved her pride. *He could have saved the damage she would do him.* But oh, no, not Michael.

Kylie placed her hands on her hips and glared up at Michael. He returned the favor as though she'd already had her revenge. She hadn't, but she planned a good measure of it.

"I don't want to know where you're all going," she said finally, glaring at all the men who had formed a brotherhood against her. Pride caused her to deny what she wanted most. "But your horses are dropping road apples in front of my shop. Who's coming around to sweep up whatever gets dragged into the floors I mopped yesterday?"

"I'll be home for supper tonight," Michael said softly as if they'd shared their lives forever.

"Have you told her yet?" Tanner asked as Michael sliced mushrooms for salad. As if waiting to go home to Kylie had made him too restless to concentrate, Tanner reached for the feta cheese and crumbled it expertly, slowly, thoughtfully into the torn lettuce.

"That I stood up in front of the Women's Council and told them of my intentions to marry her? No. I walked into her shop, found Leon sleeping on his massage bench while she was working on her customer. We had a few words, good old Leon and myself. Right now, she's not talking to me. Thanks by the way, for bringing over presentable clothes this morning—I didn't want to go to my place,'' Michael said.

''A dress shirt and tie won't help you if Kylie learns what you said to the Women's Council before you tell her. My sister's pride is ramrod straight and she can tear the truth from most men with a look, just as my mother could. My Gwyneth is on the Council. They've promised to keep your secret, but it's only a matter of time. My advice is to tell Kylie as soon as possible.'' Tanner studied the flowers Michael had placed on the table in Anna's cut glass vase. Chicken breasts with lemon and herbs waited for the skillet's olive oil to heat, the clothes washer and dryer chugged away and Kylie's sorted clothing lay on the utility floor, waiting to be laundered. Tanner frowned; a newly married man, he'd been too busy floating on air to realize how hard Kylie had been working, how little she had been caring for her own needs.

Michael's green eyes swung to Tanner's, man to man, brother to the man who would court Kylie. ''I thought I'd work into it, once she's talking to me again.''

''You meant it then, the way you love her, the way she holds your heart.'' Moments and lifetimes hung in Anna's kitchen where so many important moments had been decided. ''My sister can't bear to open her hope chest, and my Gwyneth says it's important for Kylie to meet what was and what can be.''

''Kylie will do what she needs, in her own time,'' Michael murmured. Kylie's strength was true and bold when needed. ''Your wife will be hunting for you…and me for making you late.''

Tanner thought of his wife; he'd kiss Gwyneth's pouty

lips, let the warming come gently upon them, and then the
fire— ''Have to go,'' he said abruptly, suddenly eager to
be home and hold Gwyneth tight against him.

''Tanner?'' Michael asked quietly. ''I'll take good care
of her.''

After Tanner had gone, hurrying home to his wife, Michael leaned back against the kitchen counter, sipping his
wine and watching the night settle outside. It hadn't been
easy to arrange the black Porsche for Leon's use, to talk to
the man who would let Kylie provide for him. Michael
didn't want Leon driving Kylie's pickup or utilizing any
part of her. Leon was maneuverable, though, Michael discovered, if his vanity was played on. Michael had slid the
''found a great car—but I don't need another one'' deal to
Leon as he lounged in the back of the shop, watching television. The Porsche had been a gift from a wealthy
woman—Michael had returned her kidnapped daughter.
Locked in a shed and covered with canvas, the metal beauty
represented another life to Michael, when possessions and
money ruled him. Leon merely accepted the overly low
monthly payments, no questions asked; he was certain that
soon he'd have the check he needed to leave ''this hick
town.''

Unused to waiting for others, Michael checked the salad
wilting on the counter, the chicken breasts overdone and
the pasta overcooked. He glanced at the wall phone and
damned it for not ringing, for not bearing Kylie's voice.
She was in a fine mile-high temper this morning, and later
on when he tried to talk with her. The flash of her blue
eyes had scalded him at first and then the frost set in. Taking care to lift Anna's big white apron to wipe away the
greasy smudge marks, Michael began to tap the numbers
for Soft Touches. He replaced the phone with a bang. It

was her place to be home on time, his to do the cooking, and cleaning. If she gave Leon an after-hours massage—

Michael stared at his fist, which had just banged down on the counter. He wasn't used to sweet words. Giving was in his heart, not on his tongue. She'd have to accept that of him, bend a bit, just as he was doing.

He glanced at the clock, ticking too slowly through the hour. He ran his hands through his hair, uncertain of himself now. Kylie had looked too clean and new, her hair swirling around her this morning, the sunlight sparkling in it, her eyes as clear and blue as the Montana sky. What was he doing now? Trying to present himself as something he wasn't? Michael cursed and knew he should have asked Kylie if he could speak for her— His throat went dry because he didn't fear losing his pride if she refused him; he feared driving her away.

He released the breath he'd just realized he'd been holding and scrubbed his hands roughly over his face. He'd made a mistake by stating his claim, telling Fidelity and the Council of his intentions without consulting Kylie. She'd kill him for certain, if the way she treated him when they were younger was any gauge.

At this point, he was doomed, and nothing would do but to follow the path he'd set and try to correct his error. He turned off the lights, lit the candles over which he had planned to tell her of his heart, and sat at the kitchen table. The meal was ruined and cold and so was the romantic evening he had planned when Kylie's pickup parked in the driveway.

"Where have you been?" Michael demanded as Kylie opened the back door at eight o'clock that night and pushed her tired body through it. With the kitchen candlelight behind him, his legs braced apart and his hands on his hips, Anna's big white apron didn't seem like a peace flag. Kylie

had started her day running after him when he should have
been close and warm and kissable.

"Your things. I don't want you turning up at Tanner's
and borrowing clothes. If you live here, you live *here,* not
asking Gwyneth to wash and dry for you." Kylie hurled a
black leather bag at him as she passed into the house. Her
shoulders and back ached from work, Leon had been difficult, and she could have used one of Michael's sweet
kisses, his hands soothing her. Clearly, with his scowl
drawing his brows together, the jut of his chin as appealing
as cold granite, and his mouth set in a hard line, their
moods matched. She scanned the lovely dinner that he had
cooked, the candles dripping and flickering in their glass
holders. "What are you up to, Michael Cusack?"

He dropped the bag onto a chair as if he would have
nothing between them but the truth. "Where were you?"

She'd spent the day wondering about how he had looked,
all arrogant and dressed in his jacket and borrowed dress
shirt and tie and his jeans. He'd taken care with his hair,
though the wind swept through it. Michael usually wore
casual clothes, sweaters and sweatshirts and flannel shirts
and eventually—while massaging Lorene's secretarial-stiff
shoulders—Kylie came upon the logical reason for Michael
and Tanner and the rest riding into town. Tanner's new
marriage and his treatment of Gwyneth was probably being
reviewed by the Committee for the Welfare of Brides. The
Committee kept a close watch on new marriages to set the
righteous paths for the rest of marital life. An old-fashioned
and courtly man, Tanner would do such a thing, inviting
Michael—a Cull—to the interview. "I know what you were
up to this morning. It's like my brother to be kind. Don't
count on it from me."

"Kylie, I—" he began, but the day had been too much,
weighing down on her.

"Starting out my day running after you didn't make me happy," she stated, just so he would have no doubt as to how she felt. "I'm out of shape. I've decided to exercise more and maybe take up jogging. Exercise takes away a lot of frustration. You frustrate me, Michael. But I'm over that now and if you're wanting to make peace by cooking, this is the perfect way to do it."

"Kylie, there's something we need to—"

She slid into a chair and Michael grunted darkly as she couldn't find the strength to take off her jacket. He eased it from her and filled a plate, heating it before placing the food in front of her. "Yum," Kylie murmured, distracted by the golden braised chicken and the lemon scent. She dug into the pasta, and with a mouthful of it, dug into the wooden bowl of salad. "Yum."

"So here we are, you and me," Michael said after sitting down. He watched her hurry to eat, the delicious scents reminding her of an empty stomach. He cut the chicken breast on her place, placing a bite in her mouth. "You haven't eaten all day, have you?"

"I was busy." Kylie dived for the toasted garlic bread. She didn't want to meet Michael's dark, brooding expression. She wasn't certain of herself or of him. After his morning meeting, he'd come to see her, waited for her to finish with Mrs. Morton's leg massage to drain the fluids gathering there. Just the sight of Michael set her off, and when he smiled coldly at Leon, she wasn't certain of anything. "I'm not used to explaining."

She could feel him drawing away, protecting himself, placing all those walls between them. She hurried to explain, "I went to your house to collect your things. There was a bit of cleaning to be done."

Michael stiffened and across the flickering candlelight, his narrowed green eyes seared her. "You didn't. You didn't go there after working all day and take care of them.''

"I don't want trouble, Michael, and you look like a thundercloud. They needed help. Neither one of them has taken care of themselves before. Sharon needs to eat properly. They needed clean clothes and Leon has never mastered laundry. I'm trying to help them learn before the baby comes.'' That neither was interested in learning infuriated her.

Though he was silent, Michael's anger hit her in waves. He stood abruptly, jarring the dishes on the table. Without a word, he walked to the back door and took his jacket off the hook. Anna's big apron draped around his wide braced legs, a contrast to Tanner's dress shirt and tie. "I'm going out.''

After the display of machismo with Leon this morning, Kylie feared the worst. She had to distract Michael; she wasn't too tired to keep Michael from a cold lonely night and the shadows that never seemed to be far away. "I thought we'd go down to the Silver Dollar tonight. There's not much on television.''

"You don't have to entertain me, Kylie.'' Michael tore off the apron as if it, and the dinner he'd prepared, offended him.

She'd hurt him, she realized as his hand gripped the doorknob and he prepared to escape her. Then Michael's fist tightened, the knuckles whitening as he held very still, his body taut. Then he turned back to her, his eyes gleaming. "You're not asking me for a date, are you, Kylie Bennett?''

He'd dropped her married name as if it pained him. In Freedom Valley, when searching for a bridegroom, women did the asking. Michael was in her care; she couldn't have him wandering the cold night alone—without her—or calling Leon out. In addition, she needed to find a way to tell him of the broken window at his house. Leon's weights were meant for gyms, not bedrooms. She'd managed to tape sheet foam and plastic over the window, and to clean up the kitchen while she cooked Sharon's favorite veggie and rice dish. The flickering candles, melted low upon the cut glass holders, deepened her guilt. "I'll ask them to leave. You should have your own home."

"Are you asking me for a date, Kylie?" Michael repeated very quietly and each knew the courting rules of Freedom Valley. The decisions were hers.

"Yes," she whispered, giving in to her instincts instead of her pride.

After dinner, Michael frowned as he drew on Kylie's coat. She'd been in a good mood, laughing about one of her customers as they washed and dried dishes. A man who shared little of his heart with others, Michael could not find the right moment to serve her what he had done.

It had seemed so right this morning, speaking for her in the traditional way—so wrong to have the moment dissected or shattered by too many questions. Strange how he could face a back alley brawl, outnumbered by men who intended to maim or kill him, and giving the woman he loved the truth of what he'd done was overpowering.

Kylie drove her pickup and Michael pondered the difficulty of romantic speeches to volatile women. Correct timing was chancy and fleeting. Just when he decided to make his move—to admit what he'd done—the moment passed as Kylie launched into another conversation. He should tell her of making his claim to the Women's Council. He should have—

Then the danger of his error and logic slid away as Kylie's breath slid along his cheek and her body trembled,

warm and flowing beneath his hands, finding that incredible
sweet heat upon her lips. They stopped beside a field,
watching the frost gleam beneath the moon. In her pickup,
beside him, Kylie was too close, too fragrant, too warm—
He tugged her into his arms, to see if he'd dreamed last
night, her soft sighs against his skin, those curves tucked
close and yielding to him.

Tell her, his mind told him as his body held hers tight,
his hands filling with her, hungry for her.

He dived into the summer lightning storm that was Kylie,
his heart thundering with his needs, the final need to tear
away her clothes, letting her skin burn his.

''Michael...'' she sighed in the way that pushed away
logic and served him dreams.

Tell her, his conscience whispered even as his mouth
found her breast, tasting it and the riveting waves poured
from her. *Tell her.* Then as she arched to his touch, Michael
could only feel, hear her heartbeat, want— Her hands moving over his chest and back did little to bring him to reality,
to what he must do.

Eight

When dark secrets are kept from those we love, it can do little but hurt when they come to light. It takes a generous heart to forgive and help heal that trespass, one such as my Kylie's.
—Anna Bennett's Journal

"This is heaven," Kylie crooned, lying back on her mother's couch, as Michael practiced reflexology on her feet. He shot her a warning glance when she wiggled her toes, just to see his reaction. Now, carefully following the colored chart of a foot, he looked little like the hungry man who had tugged her into the closet at the back of his shop, locking it. They had been alone, Leon showing off his new Porsche, and Kylie's next appointment had canceled. Michael had eased off her sweatshirt and had taken her breasts in that hot, desperate way. Nothing sweet and tender about all that raw male power igniting within her arms, the jolt had sizzled right down to her lower belly. "Mmm," he'd rumbled against her throat, shaking badly as she held him.

"Take me now," she'd whispered as he tore away his shirt to fold her close against him.

He'd stilled within her arms, breathing quietly against her cheek. His heavy slow heartbeat, like a leashed creature waiting to spring, rocked the closet's shadows. "Not this way, not for you."

"How then?" she'd whispered back and Michael's dark, knowing chuckle mystified her as his kisses grew more tender and enticing. In the dim light, he cupped her breasts, caressing them as he studied her.

Because she'd had him close and locked in, blocking his escape, Kylie had stripped away her sweatpants and briefs. She'd wanted him then, wanted to take him before he withdrew into reserves she didn't understand. "Well?" she'd demanded.

Michael hadn't moved, his gaze flickering down her nude body. His hands had moved toward her breasts and then, rested lightly beneath her throat. "You can't just come at a man like that," he finally whispered in a raw uneven tone.

"Why not?" she'd been curious, watching his dark hot expression, her hands over his.

"For one thing, I've got plans," he'd said hoarsely. And because he'd looked so wary and fierce and hot at the same time, Kylie had leaped upon him.

She studied the man massaging her toes now, in her mother's living room. The technique wasn't quite clinical, but more of a caress as if he wanted to study every molecule of her. Michael had to be treated gently, she decided, and he'd been unprepared for her feasting upon him. "I hope I didn't frighten you today."

His grunt said little, his eyebrows drawn in concentration

as he studied the chart. She wanted to discuss the intimacy running now between them. There had been little chance last night and this morning, when she'd walked into the kitchen to a dark brooding man who slapped a hearty breakfast on the table in front of her. "Eat," he'd said, glowering at her, the night's stubble covering his jaw as he sipped his coffee and considered her darkly.

She'd supposed he was a two-cup coffee in the morning man, one of those needing to be coaxed into the day, while she felt marvelous. Michael was delicate, she suspected, and needed reassurance. His slitted, hot looks at her could take her breath away, but she wanted action and quickly so. She wanted to rip away the rules and release whatever he held so close and tight. She couldn't have secrets between them, and she'd waited forever for the event his hungry mouth and hands promised. "So how about a date?" she'd said over breakfast, feeling bold and untouched by his brooding silence as he considered her. "Tonight? Meet me at Willa's after work?"

"Maybe" wasn't exactly a cheerful answer as he held her hand, caressing the back with his thumb. The gesture was both erotic and friendly. At the door, seeing her off, his kiss was not friendly, but it tasted just right. "I'll drop by the shop today. We need to talk," he'd said roughly, caressing her sweatpants bottom. "This isn't working out."

At Willa's earlier in the evening, Michael had growled deep in his throat when she took the check. "I asked you out, remember?"

He'd drawn into his shields again, closing her out with a cold expression. "This isn't working out," he murmured again in the cold November wind outside the Wagon Wheel. "It isn't right. I have plans and you can't afford to take me on like some orphan."

"Stop growling," she'd ordered lightly and slung her

arm around his waist because he looked dark and frustrated.
"It's a trade-off. You cooked a lovely dinner last night. I
paid for dinner tonight."

"It's not the same thing. It isn't natural for a woman to
pay a man's way. I have money," he'd said, slipping his
arm around her as they walked down the street. His nettled
pride came from his childhood when he was supporting his
dying father and yet would ask for nothing.

"Why isn't this working out?" she asked now after a
lovely meal at Willa's Wagon Wheel Café as Michael was
massaging her feet. He had baked a chocolate cake, using
her mother's cookbook, and she had leaped upon it hungrily
after their return to the house. Now, with a plate of crumbs
balanced on her stomach, and a beautiful man with strong
warm hands massaging her feet, she wallowed in her good
luck.

He studied her foot and corresponded the zones to the
colored ones on his chart.

"I'm busy here," he muttered. "This takes concentration. Let's see, this outside area by your little toe is for
your ears. This area is for heart and lungs."

As if she needed stimulation for those areas with Michael
near and scented of the chocolate cake. Experimentally, she
dipped her finger in a dollop of remaining frosting on her
plate; she sat up to ease it into his lovely mouth. The flick
of his tongue and the heated suction launched an unsteady
frustration. She wiggled her free foot up his side, only to
have it captured by the press of his arm. "Stop that. You're
distracting me."

"Are you always so intent?"

His gaze jerked to her lips, brushed her breasts and
slowly ran down her legs to the toes he was massaging.
"I'm thorough once I get started."

"I liked you nabbing me in the closet," she said, tossing

a tidbit into the beginning intimacy bin. "You don't seem like the instinctive, impromptu type."

"Sorry about that." His tone lacked sincerity.

She studied the glow of the lamplight on his lashes, the way he experimentally moved his knuckles and fingertips across the areas of her feet. Those areas at the base of her toes were energy reservoirs and even without his testing them, they leaped into alert. He frowned when he touched her heel in a way that made her knee jerk, and sensitized her femininity. She rubbed her arch on his hard thigh and Michael scowled at it. "You've got very pretty feet, but they are in the wrong place," he stated tightly.

She realized she was wiggling her toes too close to his jeans' zipper and eased them away. Michael's hands trembled as he gripped her feet in both hands, as if not knowing whether to replace them or push them away. He lifted her foot to place a kiss inside her arch, watching her. The electricity from his tongue staked every nerve and took her clawing at the couch. She found her breath and wished she could draw him over her, in her. "I know you resented me paying for dinner, but you've been working too hard. I heard you doing laundry last night. I can stop by your place and get you more clothes, if you wish."

Michael looked up from studying her foot and higher places. He gripped her ankle, not tightly, but possessively. "Do not go there again."

He frowned, studying her more closely as she looked away. "You did. You actually went there and cleaned for them again, didn't you? You probably cooked some nutritious goodie for Sharon."

"Who's Rosa?" she asked, since Michael's gentle relaxing mood was broken and whatever rode him was back and angry. His "Call Rosa for women" memo flashed in her mind on the list of things to discuss with Michael. She'd

found the note on his workbench in the back of her shop
and it had nagged her all day.

Michael shook his head. "Some woman I know," he
explained curtly. "I asked you not to clean for them."

"You didn't ask. You ordered." Kylie stood to her feet,
angry with him. He would give her nothing, not even information about a name, a woman he knew.

Michael stood slowly, towering over her like a dark thun-
derstorm brewing a good lightning bolt. "I'm going out."

"Fine. Run. Intimacy frightens you, so do relationships." She wasn't tired anymore, pleasured by Michael's
beginning reflexology techniques. "I can do my own toes."

Michael ran his hand through his hair, leaving it in peaks.
He had that desperate, trapped expression. "Kylie, I—"

"What?" She realized her tone gave him little opening
for telling her what was on his mind, but with her body's
needs on override, she wasn't happy to know she couldn't
keep the man she wanted desperately within arm's reach.

"I'm going out for a beer."

"At the Silver Dollar?" Where everyone could see that
he was still lonely and haunted and that she couldn't keep
a man she'd asked on a date?

"On the back picnic table. It's nice and cold and safe
out there."

Michael studied the bottles of colored nail polish he had
arranged neatly over his workbench the next day. They represented the dreams he had of having Kylie's full attention,
of watching her little feet play and intertwine with his as
they lay on her daffodil splattered sheets. Making love to
Kylie in a closet or in the front seat of her pickup wasn't
what she deserved. Little had kept Michael from surging
into her, placing himself deep in her, but he'd wanted an
old-fashioned bed and a marriage ring on her finger. *What*

was he doing? What made him think he was suitable marriage material for Kylie?

She knew about his young life, and he couldn't bear her sympathy. He'd made money his goal for years, skipping the intricacies of relationships and Kylie was a woman who deserved conversation and intimacy. "Don't you run away from me again," she'd called out to him as he sat brooding on the picnic table.

She'd hurried out into the wind and hurled a warm shawl around his head and shoulders. She tucked it around him tightly and pushed back the fringes from his eyes. "You're here, and it's my fault and I'm not having people say I can't take care of you. Oh, don't glower at me. You don't frighten me."

It had been odd, yet right, sitting on the old picnic table, nursing his beer and wrapped in a woman's large woolen shawl.

Leon, currently preening in the mirror, presented a problem. With Fredricka, who had stopped by to visit Michael, watching him, Leon was putting on quite a show of flexing muscles in the simple task.

"He is vain and a troublemaker," Fredricka murmured quietly before sauntering over to Leon and smiling at him. "I would like a massage. Do you take walk-ins?"

Leon eyed Fredricka's tall, statuesque body, her wide blue eyes and her long blond hair. "I think I have an opening now."

Fredricka turned to look at Michael. "I have always liked you and Kylie," she murmured. "It is good between you?"

"Pretty good." *If she weren't killing herself worrying about Leon and Sharon, and if Michael had told her of his intentions, already known to everyone else.*

"Kylie loves her work. She's not much on playing,"

Leon interrupted, not wanting to be excluded from the quiet conversation. "Except sports. She's always been a tomboy. Not very feminine. Too open. No mystery."

"Has she?" Michael asked darkly, nettled by Leon's lack of knowledge of Kylie.

"I'd hardly call her a vamp or a tigress in bed. You never see her in a dress, do you?"

On his feet now, Michael took a step toward Leon. Kylie's soft heart and her femininity weren't up for discussion. "Listen, you—"

Fredricka's hand stayed Michael. "You say you have an opening now, Leon? I've been waiting for a massage from a man with big, strong hands," she purred.

After Fredricka's tall curved body sauntered into the front part of the shop, Michael noted Leon's drool and his haste to move after her. "Freddie" was usually cool and concerned with her tulip farm and her physical shape. She usually had little time for self-indulgence, running the miles into town for her mail. Men stood by the roadside to watch her pass, a beautiful tall flow of curves and long hair who ignored them all.

Michael turned his mind from the Fredricka-mystery and concentrated on his nonexistent and painful lack of love life. Two days of hit-and-miss cuddling Kylie-sessions weren't helping his temperament, Michael decided. Honor prevented him making love to Kylie in her mother's house without a wedding band on her finger. The moment had come and gone several times in which he could tell her that he'd spoken for her at the Women's Council. It was only a matter of time before someone told her. Kylie seemed hot and ripe, and sensual tensions sprang between both of them at one look. Leon and Sharon were in the way at every turn and Kylie felt responsible for bringing them to Freedom Valley. She was too drained by running after them and

Michael could ruin whatever advances he'd made with her by just one badly needed punch— Michael opened his notebook computer, studied the various shades of polish he intended to apply with regular attention to Kylie's toes and began punching keys.

"Fredricka is awfully friendly with Leon," Kylie worried quietly at Michael's side. "You never heard me walk up to you and you're usually so perceptive. What are you doing?"

When she peered at his computer, Michael quickly exited the programs. Within hours, he intended to pry Leon and Sharon from Kylie. The responses he'd gotten from associates all over the world had been good, and Michael expected immediate confirmation of Leon's appointment at a resort far, far away.

Kylie's hand smoothed his chest and Michael almost purred aloud, pushing away the hunter's instincts that ruled him on a project. He was losing his guard, the one that had kept him alive in danger. She leaned her head on his shoulder and Michael fell into those dark blue, mysterious eyes, wondering at what ran between them, how Kylie could now be so close and warm.

Kylie had softened him, this precious little bit of curves and a cheeky grin and an open, trusting heart. She'd stolen a piece of him, but the mix of sultry, hungry woman and fairy still dazzled him. She'd fascinate him long past what brewed and sizzled between them now. He knew that she wanted him, but while he might permit a taste, he had beautiful, wild plans for the claiming of Kylie. He could give her relief and himself the pleasure of watching her go into herself, capturing those riveting sensations within her. "You asked what I'm doing? Waiting for you. Maybe I always have," he said, and watched her eyes darken as his head lowered.

Moments later, Kylie tried to place her mind and her body in the same galaxy. Michael's harsh breathing, the thumping of his heart and the desperate hunger of his mouth had once more ignited her—in the closet. She leaned limply against him, cherishing his warm trembling hands. "All better?" he asked against her forehead.

She nodded and Michael eased her from his arms and with a last searching tender kiss, opened the closet door. He eased Kylie out into the room, tugged her sweatshirt down firmly and smiled at the man gaping at them. "I heard noises," Leon said finally.

Kylie trembled, the aftermath of her feverish need for Michael, as he closed the closet door. He rested his hand on her shoulder. It was a firm grip and not a caress, as if he wasn't letting her move away from him. She flushed and hurried to explain. Kylie wasn't prepared for anyone to know how much she needed Michael. Not that Leon's opinion of her mattered, but her explanation was based on her background—in Freedom Valley passion wasn't to be flaunted openly. The Women's Council would call such behavior "unseemly." Michael could fall back into the Cull bin easily. "Now Leon, this isn't what it looks like."

"Of course it is," Michael said. "She's very sexy and demanding and needs regular attention ... Leon, I'd like you and me to be friends and I'll drop over and cook dinner. I'll just put something in the oven, so it will be ready when Sharon wakes up from her nap. But I've been wondering if you'd want to take some time off now and go for a drive?" he asked the other man as if unaffected by his steamy interlude with Kylie.

"What have you been doing to Leon?" Kylie asked furiously the next afternoon while in Michael's kitchen. Michael hadn't seen her since the closet incident; he'd been too busy with Leon and Sharon. As he passed Kylie's door last night, she'd jerked it open to glare at him. He'd smiled at her, thinking how cute she was in her flannel pajamas, her green mud mask hard upon her face, framing her vivid blue cutting eyes and her firmed pink lips. He could have tugged her to him and kissed her until that first yielding began—but he didn't. He had plans for Kylie and they included a proper consummation upon a righteous bed. When she was soft and mellow in his arms, all that fire banked for the moment, he'd tell her how he'd spoken for her. He'd tell her of his life, of the women who periodically stayed with him and some of whom he still supported as they grasped the first rung of their futures as independent women.

"You're in a froth," he had noted and wished the women he helped would have a bit of Kylie's fire and strength.

"'In a froth.' You're using my mother's words and you've got that closed, hard look. What exactly did you do to Leon?" Kylie had demanded.

Now, in the early afternoon circled by a cold mist, after setting off all the alarms Michael had reset, Kylie was furious. Her mouth tightened as she glanced at his work, cleaning up after his guests. The swishing dishwasher was filled with dirty dishes discarded throughout the house, the washer and dryer going full blast. While Leon was meticulous about the Spa's neat appearance, he discarded that trait in his off-duty hours. Sharon's attempts at cooking were evidenced by the black crust at the bottom of all of Michael's pots and pans. After one disaster, Sharon had simply moved on to another pan without cleaning the first. "Sorry about the window they broke. I'll pay for the damage," Kylie muttered.

Michael punched the buttons to stop the alarms Kylie

had started; he punched the row of remote buttons to disable them in his shop behind Soft Touches and in his vehicles. He'd wanted to see if Leon's gleaming, well-defined muscles could adjust to a good old-fashioned back-alley brawl. Leon hadn't offered to repay him for anything, and Michael wondered how much Kylie had sacrificed in her marriage. "You're not paying for anything. I haven't done anything to him. But I'd like to."

"He left a note. He's got a good job in San Francisco, managing an elite spa. The corporation has spas all over the world and it's likely that after the baby, they'll be located in Switzerland, just where he's always wanted to be. He said Sharon wanted to leave, too, and he's going to sign a contract with great employee benefits. I always knew that with just a little nudge and the right incentive, Leon would become more responsible. It was worth my effort, for the baby's sake. Why didn't you answer your telephone this morning? I couldn't leave Mrs. Watson, not after she'd taken so much care and pride in making her appointment— she's approaching one hundred, you know. I want to know what you said or did to Leon to make him and Sharon leave town so quickly. Leon usually liked to stage his good-byes, lingering over them. He didn't this time. If their using your house was too much of an inconvenience, they could have stayed at mine... And why did Sharon call, raging about the blond bionic Amazon stealing her husband? None of this makes any sense."

"Miracles happen." Michael's extensive contacts had confirmed the setup, and within a few hours had gotten Leon a high-paying job and an accompanying apartment. Leon had pounced upon the offer. Michael had slipped Leon an envelope containing cash and the signed title of the Porsche. Michael had made certain that Leon knew if he asked Kylie for money or support again, that the consequences would be "unfriendly."

Michael settled back against his kitchen counter to watch Kylie pace back and forth. Fredricka's warning look made perfect sense now. She seldom entered the life stream of others, but clearly she knew how to dispose of a man by making his wife jealous. Fredricka liked life smooth in Freedom Valley and she had apparently taken action to remove the newcomers chafing the town. Seemingly deep in thought, Kylie picked up the bottle of furniture oil and the rag he'd intended to use and went to work on the antique table. "They should have used coasters to prevent these water marks. These weren't here when I set the table that first night."

Kylie straightened and frowned and slowly studied his kitchen and the living room. "Oh, a fireplace. It's just the thing on a day like this with the blustering wind outside. Just lovely, with cream carpeting and cushions on dark heavy furniture. What a lovely view of the mountains! They're all draped in mist now— You know, I was so busy taking care of Leon and Sharon that I didn't really look at your home. The pantry and laundry room were arranged so conveniently off the kitchen and the guest bathroom is delicious. Karolina is dying for an invitation. She's certain you've got a swords display and shrunken heads."

Michael smiled tightly. His pistols and other gear were hidden in wall panels throughout the house. He imagined Karolina's glee if she were to try his night-vision, heat-sensing and voice tracking and recognition equipment. A private room, well equipped with sensors, occupied his barn's loft. Testing high-tech security devices in privacy away from labs with spies had become lucrative and he enjoyed trying his skills. "Karolina has an imagination."

He followed Kylie as she wandered from room to room,

staring at the nursery and the tiny cots provided for visiting children. "I'd like children someday," he said. "Would you?"

"You ordered new things for the women and the children. Why?"

He shrugged, unable to tell her of how dark those lives had been. "They were my friends and they needed things."

Kylie studied him, placing her hand along his jaw. "Michael, no one will think less of you for having a giving heart. Don't be ashamed of the good you do. That you've always done."

He wanted to tell her about his mother, about Lily and why he had chosen his path to help other women. But the words were locked tight in his throat; he wasn't used to giving away parts of his life. It was a trait he intended to mend for Kylie.

He kissed her palm, nuzzled it, unable to tell her of the fullness in his heart. *Tell her, you fool. Tell her of your past and what you've done. Give her roses and wine and a dinner she'll remember. Don't let your body rule your head, not now, not with Kylie.* Had he ever let the need for a woman rule him? *Never.* The denial slapped at him as he toyed with a curl.

"I would like children," Kylie answered as the currents ran strong and warm between them. She pushed open the door to his guest room, warm with sunshine and Anna's quilts and fragrant herbs tucked into vases. "Those are my mother's braided rag rugs and her quilts. Did she stay with you?"

He thought of the long night sessions with women too shattered to trust a man, of the nights when Anna could be heard crooning to them, sleeping with them. He thought of the babies she'd brought into the world, teaching him what she knew. "Yes. She stayed sometimes."

Kylie hurled herself against him, holding him tight. ''I miss her. There was no time to say good-bye.''

He smoothed her back and nuzzled the fragrance of her hair. Anna had left lovely gifts wherever she went, caring for those she loved and those who needed her. ''She's here. In you and Tanner and Miranda.''

Kylie burrowed her face against his throat. ''I'm not like her, not as sweet and good, especially when it comes to you.''

Michael fought the shiver of his need, that careening of tenderness into sensual need, to claim her as his own. He pushed away an unfamiliar foolish grin, which had just startled him.

She looked up at him and smoothed his hair and the shadows inside Michael went tilting into soft and fuzzy. ''You'll be moving back to your home. You probably only moved in to protect me. Leon had wanted to become…friendly again. Stop muttering. He was only feeling a little insecure.''

'''Insecure,' my—'' Michael bit off the rest of his curse. He had to tell Kylie soon. Rosa had called him about ''Jeanne,'' her last name customarily ignored. Legal restraining orders hadn't prevented her husband's abuse and she was heavily pregnant, the baby endangered. For the time being Jeanne was indecisive, but once she made up her mind for protection, Rosa would need a safe house for her. ''Mmm. I've got a problem and your mother's house isn't the place for it.''

''No? You're not comfortable?''

''I'm very uncomfortable.'' He eased back a wind-tossed curl, still cool from the mist outside, and traced her ear, thinking how perfect she was. ''I still see her there, and I've got plans for her little girl.''

''Oh?'' There was just that challenging tilt of her head,

that slanted blue look, daring him to explain. "I can't see that it matters."

"I do." Michael tugged her to him and took, dived into her, tasted all the sense of coming home, mixed with earth and violets and woman. Stunned momentarily, her lips first resisted the tug of his teeth, then parted to deepen the kiss. She fisted his hair, hoarding him, the air charging with tiny flashes of lightning, bouncing off the hallway as he held her feet above the floor, carrying her.

He'd only intended to give them each relief, to touch Kylie, reassuring himself of her response to him, that unshakable trust and honesty. But she'd caught him broadside, fiercely opening herself to him and his instincts to take her leaped into life. He'd take just a little, he promised himself, to soothe what ran between them. He'd stop—

He fell with her onto the bed, hurrying to skim the soft curves and heat that was Kylie. Her hands slid beneath his T-shirt, tearing it upward, tossing it away. He fought for caution, to tell her of his life, to tell her that he'd spoken for her, but then she fussed at his jeans. Unable to work the snap, she held him and her tremble ran through him, became his.

"Did *they* sleep here?" she whispered once, desperately as he hurried with their clothing, freeing them.

He should stop. He should tell her everything. But his blood rushed on feverishly, demanding he take what was his, the woman of his heart and soul. This would be where he would take his love, Michael thought as the fever pushed through his body, here in the dim shadows with the scent of mist clinging to her, the past and the future waiting to be bonded.

He traced her breast, cherishing it, slowly tasting her flesh. He'd seen her briefly in the closet, her curves shadowed, but that glimpse hadn't prepared him for the gleam-

ing pale flow of silky skin, the dips and hollows and the—
He sucked in air, smoothing the flat of his hand over her
stomach, tracing the jut of her hipbones. "No. I kept it
locked. No woman has ever been here, with me, but you."
Kylie…Kylie. He gently eased away her jacket and looked
down at her, losing himself in her dark blue gaze, the heat
pouring from her.

"Mmm, freckles," he murmured against her throat, finding the ripeness of her breast, cherishing the heated press
of her body, her bare legs twining restlessly against his.

"Yum," she whispered back, stroking his chest, igniting
the tempest within him. He heard his laughter, wild and
free, and wondered how he could release such emotion,
such joy.

Kylie rolled over him, rocked her hips against him. She
cried out helplessly, and her soft, waiting flesh pressed
against the hardness of his body. He couldn't have her take
him so easily, taking her riotous hair in his hands. This was
his taking of the woman who had his heart and he had to
meet her hunger, deny her nothing. Yet the darkness within
him prowled, needing the capture. He fought back the primitive need to sink deep within her, to take and take and
take. Kylie's fingernails dug into his shoulder and her teeth
latched to his throat for a tiny wound. "Don't you dare,
Michael Cusack. Don't you dare think of good and right
and honor."

"Oh, I wasn't thinking of that, dear heart," he whispered, not bothering to keep the humor from his tone.

"Well, then?"

"It's the doing that needs to be good and right and
proper."

Impatient for him, Kylie shook his shoulders and the
gentle etch of her peaked nipples against his chest, the heat
rising from her took him to the cusp, his primitive need for

his mate driving him over her. Taking a heartbeat for protection, Michael found her breasts with his open mouth.
She cried out then, just as fierce as he, her legs capturing
his. Tearing away layers of time and restraint, driving to
the wild hunger pounding between them, Kylie helplessly
watched Michael's desperate expression.

This was his love, his heart, his home, her face flushed
with desire, her dark blue eyes widening as he entered her
very carefully. He seemed almost grim and yet desperately
locked in the passion between them, his body trembling as
he braced his full weight from her. "That's it. Keep your
eyes open, baby."

"Yes." *Yes, my love, for I can do nothing else but watch
the beauty between us.*

A wild flush rose in his dark cheeks and as his fierce
gaze ripped down their entangled bodies, she knew he was
locking the image in his mind. When he turned back to her,
his expression was tender.

This is my first time, Kylie mused. *No other has gone
before, nor ever will go again. Not like this, with my Michael.* His hands were linked with hers, palms hard and
callused, fingers strong and yet not hurting. She paused
there in the first of their joining, holding her mind apart for
just that heartbeat, before she gave herself to the fury. There
would be no going back, no hiding what she felt, for she
had decided to feast upon him, take what she wanted. She'd
waited a lifetime for him, Kylie decided as Michael's face
hardened, his eyes dark and mysterious upon her. She'd
remember the rough crisp cut of his hair, the way he
breathed, just that slight flaring of his nostrils as if he was
taking her into him, just as her body accepted him. He was
a part of her now, lodged deeply, frowning in his concern,
still taking care to hold his weight apart, not to hurt her.
There was just the slash of light gleaming on his cheek-

bones, his mouth slightly swollen from their kisses. It was a beautiful mouth, she decided and fit for a small boy who looked just like him. She listened to the beating of her heart, the thud of his, and gave herself to being one with Michael. He'd come home to her, filling her. Completed now, fully joined, she sighed and closed her eyes, taking in, remembering how it was now with Michael trembling and hot and hungry and his eyes burning down upon her. She inhaled his scent, that of wood smoke and soap, and storms wild and free and burning away everything else.

"Am I hurting you?" His voice shook with emotion, his eyes bright with it, as if it poured out of him, shaking the shadows around them.

"No, you're not. It's just so beautiful." Then she opened her eyes to Michael, caught his concern and lifted her lips to ease his fears. "Take me," she whispered in that dim shadowy room, amid the scent of freshly washed sheets, rain and Michael. Amid the future and the past and the leaping fire between them. She intended to tear his heart from him, to make him hers. She arched, ready to set about her work and her pleasure, and give him everything.

Ah, Kylie, love, you're fearless and wild. You're too small and fierce and determined to take us both too quickly.

Then Michael's thoughts were torn away by his passion, by the woman claiming him, and by his taking of her. She rose and fell beneath him as smoothly as a warm wave, her hair spread out upon his pillow, her eyes narrowed as if she were closing in—her body echoed the tremors deep within, and Michael was lost, hurled into the red rockets bursting inside his head.

He'd cried out, giving himself to her, and through the slow clenching of her body, Kylie forced her eyes open to see him, her captive, her lover. The unique sense of being well-loved flowed through her, as she floated down to earth, Michael resting upon her. She stroked his back, damp as

her own flesh, for they had burned in fire. She listened to
his uneven breath and smiled as she sensed him trying to
reclaim himself. She couldn't have that, letting him draw
back into his shields and his shadows. "Michael?" she
murmured against his ear and floated when he lazily caressed her breast.

"Mmm. I'll move—" His voice was dark and deep and
drowsy, enchanting her.

She held him tight, locked upon her. She wasn't letting
him get away, not after her first experience with the ultimate sensual pleasure. "Don't you dare."

"I'm heavy, love. Let me move aside."

She flicked her tongue against his ear, felt the jolt of his
reaction deep within her body. She'd have him again and
on her terms. "If that's all there is—"

He raised up on an elbow, scowling at her, his hair wild
from her hands. She grinned up at him and slid him another
torment, because Michael could be arrogant when he chose
and she couldn't have that. "Was this a sampler?"

She delighted in his dazed, stunned look. It quickly
changed to desire and she reveled in the changing of his
expressions, the hardening of his body as he took her again.

By evening, the mist had become rain, pattering gently
on the windows, and Michael watched Kylie sleep in his
arms, curled trustingly against him. She had the look of a
kitten, of a child he remembered from long ago, yet the
brush of her breast against his side took his thoughts to the
fiery woman she'd become, matching his needs, tearing him
away.

He had to tell her, he thought, even as he turned her
gently, kissing away her drowsy protest. He smiled against
her lips, now warming to his. She sighed luxuriously,
dreamily, her body welcoming him as he slid within.

Nine

A baby comes new and fresh into the world, cleansing and giving bright hope. Truth usually comes then, and grows with that tiny, new life.
—Anna Bennett's Journal

He had to tell her. He'd been a fool to unleash his passion for her before she understood his heart and his intention. Michael breathed in Kylie's scents, their earthy warm scents combined and haunting him in his bedroom. She curled against him, exhausted and trusting. Marking the times they'd made love, bluish shadows glowed beneath her closed lids, her face pale within her tousled, wild hair. The easy sweep of her breath across his throat caused him more fear than confidence. Rain streamed down the windows, leaving patterns upon her pale face, her eyes shadowed by exhaustion. A cold wash of fear paralyzed him;

he could lose her easily this dreary morning, with the wrong words or actions.

He had not cared about other women. They'd long ago faded by time and by his need of Kylie that burned bright and hardened his body even now, after they'd made love several times. For Kylie, he had to make this morning right, to correct his failure to tell her about asking for her and about his life.

She'd come at him once, surprisingly strong, her sleek muscles stronger than he'd suspected as she'd moved over him, taking him within. She'd been glorious then, fighting him and diving into her passion, tearing away everything else but what ran true and wild between them at that moment—

Desperation and fear thundered through him as he wondered what would please a woman the morning after they'd made love. It hadn't mattered before; he'd never stayed the night. He'd never wondered if he were romantic enough, tender enough.

Kylie stirred against his bare shoulder, burrowing her face against him. Tangled in her soft limbs, Michael feared waking her, but he couldn't think clearly with her so near. Gently he eased her aside and slid from bed. He showered away from his bedroom, letting the hot water sluice over him, trying to grasp what he must do, what he must say. He skipped calling the florists for a delivery of roses— Freedom was a small town and Kylie's honor had to be kept. He settled for digging through a gift box of sea salts and bubble bath sent to him by Rosemarie, a woman now on her own but grateful for his help. He'd heard Anna speak of the calming use of chamomile tea and brewed a cup for Kylie, then foraged through Rosemarie's box until he found a small vial labeled Chamomile de Bain.

He hurried to the bathroom adjoining his bedroom, ran

Kylie's bathwater, checked its heat and planned the breakfast he intended to serve her. His thoughts careened
wildly—he had to give her something, but there was nothing. Another man would have had his mother's ring to give,
a sweetheart necklace, or pearl earrings, tiny and perfect
for Kylie's small ears. He had no family treasures; he'd had
no family to cherish. He'd set his goals to survive, to become financially secure. Reassured that he'd never again
live in poverty, hunger clawing at his belly, he'd settled
into a life that was safe. He found mild excitement in testing security systems and rewarding pleasure when he could
help women like his sister.

No more than a small lump of curves in his bed, Kylie
stirred and sighed. Michael paused in midstep, fearing that
she would awake and he'd have nothing to give her.
"Yum," she murmured, snagging his pillow against her,
and Michael knew he'd better hurry. Kylie was always in
a better mood when well fed.

He had little time, before she awoke and he hurried to
the kitchen, breaking eggs with shaking hands. He slathered
butter and raspberry jam on her toast, and made another
cup of chamomile tea because the first had grown cold. He
was just filling the tray when Rosa called. Jeanne had
fought her last battle and wanted peace and a new life for
her baby. Michael glanced at the clock and knew he had
little time to tell Kylie.

A second call from Karolina grimly reminded him that
he had planned to make thoughtful, careful love to Kylie.
"You bought enough for a year, according to the druggist.
You'd better be treating my friend right, Michael Cusack,
or I'll—"

She gasped when Michael interrupted, "Butt out, Snoop.
I'm taking care of her. We're doing this trial marriage
thing."

"She doesn't know that! You'd just better tell her what you did, Fast Hands. You'd better tell her that you spoke your intention at the Women's Council. In fact, I'll tell her myself. She ought to know what a jerk you are. Any man who had enough nerve to go in front of the Women's Council and ignored the one little fact of telling the woman— the bride-to-be—that he had spoken for her, deserves whatever Kylie can throw at you—plates, bricks, whatever. This is a two-way deal, and you took her thunder. A woman is supposed to know this so she can wallow in what everyone says, blush a little and swish around in a pretty dress. Kylie has been wearing sweatsuits. She's not going to be happy, Fast Hands."

Michael relied on a time-proven method to shut up Karolina. "Do you want me for yourself, sweetheart?"

The disconnect buzz followed her gasped "Dog." With that minor success, Michael grinned and set about defining just what would appeal to Kylie this morning. He mentally foraged through the gifts he wanted to give her later and started working.

Kylie sighed luxuriously in the bubble bath and forced herself to rise from it. She quite simply loved Michael, for his tenderness and his care of her, for his hunger and the trembling, reverent way he touched her. She'd heard him take a shower, but she'd been too achingly exhausted to rise and— She smiled softly and thought of other mornings they would have and how she'd soap and tend Michael's hard, lean body.

His muffled shout of release had shocked him, as though he'd been tossed over an edge he hadn't expected. Then there in the brooding silence before they began again, Michael's thoughts had stalked him. A private man, he would take his time telling her whatever nagged at him.

She slid aside the mirror to search for toothpaste and frowned at the odd assortment of fingernail polish bottles, all unopened and in various shades. She pushed away the slight burn of jealousy; she'd known Michael had other women. She closed the mirror and her thoughts of Michael touching other women. The morning was too glorious and ripe with expectations to be ruined.

She stretched and yawned and noted the well-loved woman in the steamy mirror. The curl of her lips said she'd been pleasured. Her eyes were dark with the mystery of life, as if all her rivers ran smooth as warm cream, pooling gently in her relaxed muscles. The tender aches were her victory, for she had claimed pleasure, taken it into her, and returned the gift. There was more than their bodies' hunger between them. That truth rang through her as she toweled dry and slipped on his flannel shirt, carefully placed out for her. Michael had definite possibilities, she decided, and followed the lovely aroma coming from the kitchen.

She found him there, jaw dark with morning stubble, wild hair tousled by her fingers and dusted with flour. Dressed only in boxer shorts, he paced nervously back and forth across the kitchen floor, also dusted with flour. Oven mittens were an odd contrast for a big man, corded with muscles. The kitchen warrior muttered to himself, stooped to peek into the oven and muttered again. He ran a finger down an open recipe book, glared at the clock and checked the oven again. He glanced at the lovely tray he'd prepared, tested the warmth of the cup with his finger and glared at it. "She should have china and all I have is stoneware. I am not prepared for this. I am not ready and what if—"

"Michael?" If he hadn't appeared so distressed, pacing his lair, she might have laughed. The slightly reddish marks on his shoulder and back reminded her that she had dived into him and had taken. She decided to taste and kiss those slight wounds and apologize while doing so. He reacted so nicely to her mouth against his skin, his body.

Michael pivoted like a gunslinger caught off guard, glaring at her. "Go back to bed. I'm not done here."

He fascinated her, simply enchanted her as he stood there glaring at her, legs wide spread, bare chest dusted with the flour that ranged from the countertop to the floor and back again. He tore the oven mittens from his hands and tossed them aside when she leisurely leaned against the counter to snatch a slice of bacon. "It's cold. Everything is ruined. Give me a break, Kylie."

"What's up?" she asked, and tried to smother a grin.

"The damned pie takes forever. Apple. First you have to roll out this dough—I've watched Anna use a rolling pin often enough, but the damned thing is too complicated. Pie dough is delicate, you know. It tears. The apples turn dark if you're not fast enough."

"'Delicate,' like you? I'd say that at times, you're very firm."

He stared at her blankly, as if she'd just jumped galaxies. "Don't start with me, Kylie. I'm trying my best here."

She flicked the flour from the hair on his chest and thought how lovely he looked. She couldn't resist teasing him and tucked a strip of bacon into his mouth. He chewed it as though it were leather. He glared at her, a man with flour clinging to the peaks of his hair.

"Would you just go back to bed and let me handle this?" he asked in the wary, frustrated tone that could delight her.

"Yum," she purred, taking in all that long, lean body, those powerful legs and rippled stomach and beautiful muscled chest. Then because she was feeling sensually powerful and feminine and wanted to distract Michael from his frustration, she tore open the borrowed shirt and flashed him.

He gaped quite beautifully, as if his mind had gone blank, and she loved him more. Then as if it took all his control, Michael closed his eyes, trembled and the dark flush upon his cheeks dimmed. When his eyes opened again, they were slitted and shielded and brooding. "We have to talk…. That day we rode into town, I went before the Women's Council and spoke my piece for you."

Now, I've done it, Michael thought as he watched Kylie draw together the edges of his shirt, covering her body, her face paling with shock.

"What?" She shook her head as if she hadn't heard, hadn't understood him. *"What?"* she asked again, her hand closing around the cup of chamomile tea.

Perhaps her chamomile bath hadn't worked, hadn't calmed her enough. A quick glance at the oven said it would be minutes before he could serve her pie. He recognized that taut stance, those blue, angry eyes burning him. He had only a few minutes before she exploded. For a woman with a loving heart, Kylie left nothing to question when she was angered. "Drink your tea, Kylie. Sweetheart. Dear heart. Now, Kylie. I meant to tell you. I meant to do things the right way, and then I just decided to do it."

"Without telling me." Her voice was too quiet now, deadly.

Michael ran his hands through his hair, realized that the burning smell was coming from the pie he'd hoped to serve her. He jerked on the oven mittens and bent to take the pie from the stove. Latticed on top and simmering in butter, sugar and cinnamon, it had not burned, but merely bubbled over onto the bottom of the oven. "Treacherous, damned things," he muttered, thinking more of his heart than the pie.

"Michael?" Kylie asked too quietly. "What did you say to them—the Women's Council?"

"Nothing is going right," he said to himself, as his morning after making love to Kylie went sliding into the flour at his bare feet. "I said the usual things. Welcomed the Committee for the Welfare of Brides to make their inspection."

He'd been embarrassed then by the depth of love he could feel, by the future he'd dreamed of with Kylie. Even now, with her, the words were stuck tightly in his throat. But then, with Fidelity nodding encouragement, the words had begun to flow and when he was finished, he wondered why the women were teary. They were odd phrases, unfamiliar and tumbling over his tongue, much like he'd heard other men speak of their loves. He'd called her his "Sunshine" and his "morning dew," his "buttercup" and his "rose." There was something about holding her hand and watching the sunset when they were both gray and rocking on their front steps. He wished he could snag something of what he'd said now, as Kylie seemed to shimmer in the kitchen's morning light, her hair frothing around her like a silky storm.

"All this time everyone knew, but me?"

Clearly, the discussion wasn't going well as noted by the rising hitch in Kylie's tone. "I wanted to give you more time," Michael stated quite logically, he thought. He folded his arms and leaned back against the counter, watching her. He wasn't taking back anything he'd said. "But I couldn't wait. I'm usually pretty methodical about getting what I want, but with you, nothing is expected. There was Leon, using you, and the gossip, and it seemed the right thing to do. I haven't done many right things in my life, but I knew that morning, that speaking for you was what your father would have done in the same situation. I respected him and my decision was logical."

"Oh, it was, was it?" she asked before hurling the cup

at him. Michael dodged as it went hissing by him, only to clatter against the kitchen counter and fall to the floor.

The saucer followed and Michael caught it, carefully placing it aside. "It's done," he stated, wanting his love to know he cared enough for her to make a fool of himself.

"Yes, it is," Kylie agreed with a hard jolt of finality, his shirt fluttering around her thighs as she stalked back to his bedroom.

"Look, princess. You're not going anywhere until we get this ironed out," Michael said as he watched her furiously tug on her clothing.

"Try and stop me," she returned, punching him in the stomach as she passed.

Michael snagged the back of her sweatshirt and hauled her back to his scowl. "I made you a pie. I got emotional that morning, okay? I woke up at Anna's and thought how you should have a home just like that and I wanted— My first pie…you're my first and it's damned hard to be reasonable with you in a snit. You'll stay and eat it and we'll talk this out."

"Oh, will we?" she asked and delivered another punch that took his breath away. "Let me go. I'll need time to think of all the ways I'm going to murder you."

When she tromped out of his house, Kylie scooped up his pie in a dish towel and left with it and his heart.

Kylie sat on the floor, cross-legged, cuddling the warm pie that Michael had baked for her. She dug her spoon into the flaky crust, the juicy cinnamony apples and ignored the ringing telephone as she ate. "Pick up this call, dear heart," Michael growled into the message machine.

"When I'm ready." He could be so lovely one minute and unbelievable the next. Kylie sighed and allowed the brimming tears to drop into her pie. She stirred them into the sweet mixture, not hungry for anything but Michael's arms. She's asked him for a date, but then in Freedom Valley, any woman could ask for dates, a custom usually reserved for men. She'd planned to work up to more dates and asking him for the last dance, another custom to define the man a woman chose as a husband. He'd just swept right ahead into asking for her—without her knowledge. He'd acted like an old-fashioned drover that day, riding into town with her on the back of his horse. He'd made her choose him there in the frost and the steam from the prancing horses, in front of men she'd known all her life. *And she hadn't known he was asking for her!*

The next call, she heard the rasp of his morning stubble against the telephone as the machine took his message. "We just need some fine-tuning. I'm not going to apologize for speaking for you. Look, maybe it is a little quick. You're making a new life. I want to be part of it. It seems to me that we've wasted enough time. Answer this call, Kylie. I've got to go and I want this settled."

His temper and frustration were brewing and so were hers.

The morning after making love with Michael, she should have been still in his arms, locked away from the world. But she wasn't. She was dealing with the wasted past and the future and tumbling emotions she hadn't expected. She'd wanted to be feminine for Michael and he hadn't seen her in anything but sweat clothes and jeans. She'd given little to the customs of Freedom Valley and Michael had taken steps that she knew had cost him. He wasn't a man to explain his feelings and that's what the Women's Council would have demanded of him. She should have been supportive, encouraging him, and he hadn't let her. Kylie ignored another call from him, noting the desperation. "I've got to go away, Kylie. We've got to talk."

She jerked up the telephone. "Hey, buddy. You're a little late with that offer. I trusted you. You missed a step or two. Like a discussion with me."

"I haven't had that much experience, dear heart. Give me a break." His impatience rasped over the line. "I need to see you."

There was a long thoughtful pause and then Michael noted slowly, "It's because you aren't directing the relationship, because you like to be in control and you weren't, isn't it?"

She'd always had to take charge of decisions, be responsible for both herself and Leon. But the word "control" snagged.

"Now, get this, princess. I'm not your ex-husband. I know this happened fast, but— If you need time to transfer—"

"Transfer? *Transfer?* Like in ownership papers?" she demanded sharply. She'd never experienced the heights of ecstasy that Michael had given her, and he had just used business language to define what ran hot between them. "I could have worn a dress that day, Michael. It's a big day in a girl's life when a man goes before the Women's Council."

"A dress? What's that got to do with anything?" His frustration rasped through the line.

She wanted to be romantic, to be feminine and to please him. She'd been known as a tomboy most of her life, and now she wanted all of Freedom Valley to know that Michael had chosen a feminine woman. She knew that wasn't the important part of a relationship, that her logic had to do with Leon's insults. Yet silly and frivolous, it was important to her. "Some things are important, Michael. You've never seen me in a dress."

"Well, hell," he muttered, as if trying to place Venus in

alignment with Mars and the New York Mets in the Pee Wee children's leagues.

"The pie is good," she said, because in Freedom Valley, manners were important. Then she disconnected the line, which wasn't exactly sweet.

Kylie scanned the shadows of her mother's home, always so safe and warm, and knew it was time to examine her own life, to give Michael the tenderest part of herself. Were the dreams of filling her own home still there? The ones she'd placed in her hope chest and ignored for years? Was this how her mother had felt long ago, courted by her father?

She took his pie into the kitchen, placing it in her mother's pie safe. Was it true that when a girl in Freedom Valley embroidered and dreamed of love and a home all her own, that dream would come true?

Kylie rose up the steps to her bedroom, carefully removed her childhood dolls and the doily covering her hope chest. Neatly folded above her own work were three baby blankets her mother had made, the stitches tiny and placed with love. Kylie drew them out, hugged them close against her, then reached for the envelope marked "Kylie, my youngest."

The lovely paper shook in Kylie's hands as she read. "Kylie. If you are reading this, you've come home. I hope to see your face when you see the blankets I've made for my grandchildren. Miranda and Tanner each have their own and I made three for each of you, as a reminder of how close all of you were, my dear children. Instincts move you and that is good because you sense what is right. Trust yourself, Kylie, and what is beautiful and giving in your heart. You live with laughter and, in you, I see a part of myself, the need to heal and give to others. Treasure most of all, who you are and what you bring to your love. Unless all the signs are wrong, one man has given his heart to you long ago and I venture to say, he'll fill these blankets soon enough, once you agree. You were made to be cherished and loved and to fill a home with happiness and a family. When love really comes to you, it will sweep you off your feet and you'll claim him for your own before he has a chance to escape. Kiss my grandchildren for me, Kylie, and know that I am with you always. I love you. Mom.''

An hour later, Karolina threw pebbles against Kylie's upstairs window. With a groan, Kylie knew her friend wouldn't be ignored. Only a few years ago, Karolina had climbed up that big oak tree beside the house and crawled across a limb. Kylie scrubbed away her tears, her mother's journals spread on the bed beside her, each one telling of Anna's love of her family and the people in Freedom Valley. "Men are rogues," her mother had written, as if she'd been thinking of Michael. "Boys and men and beasts in one mad frustrating package. Tenderness can be shielded, and sometimes it's up to us to make sense of their maddening ways. It's for women to sort out how men touch our hearts and what runs true within us.''

Downstairs, Kylie jerked open the door for her friend. "I'm having a conversation with Mom. Go away.''

Karolina, hunched against the cold wind, blinked. "Huh?''

She recovered quickly, shoving past Kylie. "You've been crying. I knew it. I just knew that jerk would hurt you. He's leaving now. Just slid out of town in that big black rig of his, like he does when he brings back one of his women.''

"They are his friends,'' Kylie managed through a throat clogged with tears.

"You're defending him? You don't even want to know what he does when he's away? Come on, let's follow him."

Half an hour later, Kylie grumbled, "I don't know why I let you talk me into things."

She huddled in the passenger seat of Karolina's tiny car. If Michael were headed for another woman, that meant that she hadn't satisfied him. She didn't know if she could bear the blow to her pride. "Have you thought of getting another hobby, Karolina?"

"Grump. That's his taillights up there and his license plate. Now all we have to do is follow him."

Four hours later, the small town in Wyoming gleamed wet beneath the streetlights. In a shabby neighborhood, Michael's four-wheeler pulled into a small, overgrown driveway, near a tiny house. Karolina turned off her headlamps and pulled onto the opposite side of the street. "Good view."

"I don't like this." What was Michael doing? Why had he driven here? What if he did have another woman, coming to her after making love to Kylie? She couldn't bear to see him hold another woman, to kiss her.

Beaded by rain, another late model car was parked beside a battered pickup. The house lights were all on, outlining the woman who ran to meet him. In the dim light her face was hauntingly beautiful, framed by long glossy hair. He hugged her briefly and a fist clenched around Kylie's heart as Michael's head bent intimately to the woman's. From the concealing shadows of brush, Kylie watched Michael and the woman walk up the steps. A man jerked open the door and from the raging set of his powerful body, he was angry. He rammed a punch at Michael and somehow Michael dragged him from the steps as the woman entered the house.

Kylie had never seen pure rage, pure anger, a bully tear-

ing after Michael. She couldn't move, her heart bloodless.
Michael easily sidestepped the beefier man's blows, and
with one cutting motion of his hand took the bully to the
wet ground. The man lunged to his feet, pounding at Michael, who moved agilely aside. Even in the dim light, and
inexperienced in viewing brawls, Kylie noted the back alley
standards of the man. She shivered, unable to move, realizing suddenly how Michael had lived, how he'd survived.
An experienced fighter, Michael easily stepped aside to
down the man again. In the dim light, Michael's face was
harsh as he crouched beside the man, speaking to him. The
violence in his expression terrified her.

Then the woman came out, sheltering another heavily
pregnant woman within her arms, easing her into Michael's
vehicle. While Michael continued to talk to the man, the
woman ran back into the house, carrying out two suitcases.
Michael rose and took them from her, easily hefting them
into the rear of his vehicle. The beautiful woman stood near
and protective as he made another trip into the house, returning with two small boxes. Then he turned to the man
struggling to his feet. The look on Michael's face was cold
and deadly as he placed his boot on the man's throat. The
man nodded when Michael stopped speaking.

Kylie swiped at the tears in her eyes. The scene explained itself: a woman needed protecting and Michael was
there for her. He'd told her of his sister, Lily—how she'd
died unprotected. This was what Michael did in remem-
brance of Lily. Michael's fierce expression, the efficient
movements of his body, told her that he was well trained
in brawling. Yet he'd handled her so carefully, the effort
costing him, the tension running through his expression and
his body. She hadn't fully realized how powerful and lethal
he could be, yet with her—

As if they'd run through the same savage scenario many

times before, the beautiful, stately woman nodded and slid into her car, driving away. Michael backed away from the house and Karolina's excited speculations ran throughout the four hours to Freedom Valley. Finally, Kylie had enough. It had taken her a full hour to recover from the violence at that small house. This was the man he didn't want her to see, the violent man ready to protect an endangered woman. He didn't want her to see what lurked in his past, and Kylie bit her lip, remembering the wounds on his body. He'd held her reverently in the night, his body trembling, holding that full primitive violence away from her, because he was afraid he would be like his father, a brute.

"Oh, Michael, you could never be that," she whispered as the windshield wipers *click-clacked* through the memories of his lovemaking. He'd feared hurting her, not trusting himself. "When we get to Michael's, you are to let me off and you are to go home and say nothing."

Michael had known he was being followed and he suspected Karolina was the culprit. He didn't have time to stop and challenge her; he had to take care of the woman he'd retrieved. Michael's hands tightened on the steering wheel. Jeanne's contractions had started and Dr. Thomas White was on his way. At Michael's house, he eased Jeanne from the car and carried her into the house. He glanced at the lights veering off the road, outlining the woman running to him.

"This is Jeanne," he said quietly as Kylie hurried after him into the guest room. Her eyes were wide and he recognized the quivering edge of shock. He had no time to explain. How could he? How could he tell her that he was best suited to destroy? "She needs help. Her baby is coming now, too fast, and it's her first. Her water broke earlier, the contractions close together. She's probably already dilated. She didn't want to stop at a hospital. Rosa told her she would be safe with me.''

Once she'd heard the woman cry out, Kylie hadn't asked questions. She'd simply acted just as Anna had, moving to give comfort. She squeezed Michael's arm and searched his hard face, finding the fear in it that he would fail. ''Michael, I saw everything at the house. That man— She needs a doctor.''

He closed his eyes for one brief heartbeat. He'd known there was another person in Karolina's vehicle, but he'd prayed it wasn't Kylie. He'd been followed by Karolina before, and he knew that if he'd walked toward them, she would have squealed her tires, sailing off into the night. He'd had no time to deal with his fears then, because Jeanne's husband had come at him, raging and cursing. Kylie had seen what he was—who he was, tough, savage, too skillful at fighting.

''A doctor is on the way, but I can do the job, barring complications. Your mother taught me and Dr. Thomas White has his own reasons for helping. He's driving here now, and we'll be talking over the telephone,'' Michael returned grimly as he placed the woman on the bed. In her pain, Jeanne batted at his hands, and showing more age than his years, Michael turned to Kylie. ''She doesn't want a man's hands on her.''

''Hello, Jeanne. I'm Kylie,'' her voice ran smooth and warm as she gently pushed Michael from the room. She undressed Jeanne and slid a gown onto her bruised body. When Michael reentered the room, his expression concerned and frustrated, Kylie understood instantly. ''Because of your sister?''

He nodded grimly. ''Lily married the same kind of man as my father. Restraining orders don't always work. That's where Rosa and I come in. If everything else fails, we move to save the woman's life and give her a new one. All we can do is make the offer, but it has to be her decision. There are others helping along the way.''

Jeanne cried out and her hand tightened painfully on Kylie's. ''Well, then. We've got work to do, don't we, Jeanne? You know, at one time my mother brought most of the babies into Freedom Valley. She was a midwife and a good one, too. People tell me I'm like her and that's why I know that you and I are going to do a good job with this baby. My mother taught Michael, too, and he's not going to let anything happen to you or your baby. A doctor will be here soon, and we can call him at any time,'' Kylie murmured quietly, smoothing back the woman's damp hair. She began to massage Jeanne's swollen belly, amazed at the new life waiting to be born. ''Soon you'll have a tiny part of you, the best part, to hold and to love and your baby will be safe.''

She turned to Michael, and found tears shimmering in his lovely eyes. ''Tell me what to do, Michael. And, by the way, I love you.''

Ten

After a lover's storm, there is nothing like the making up and love goes on, stronger than before.
—Anna Bennett's Journal

"You've done fine work, the both of you. I'll take care of her now," Thomas White said. His smile was warm, his black hair—winged by gray—swept away from his narrow, aristocratic face. Stiletto lean and dressed in a three-piece suit, he was obviously wealthy. His rich, melodic voice lilted with an accent Kylie could not define. He held the new baby boy that Michael had just delivered, a touch of pride in his grin. "Good job, my friend. Go on now before you fall of exhaustion and break something I have to mend."

Jeanne, exhausted and happy, her eyes aglow caught Kylie's hand. "Thank you both."

Michael nodded, but one look at him, and Kylie knew

that for all his cool coaxing during the birthing, he was
deeply moved. He stood, all angles and open hands at his
side, clearly spent. The harsh lines set more deeply in his
face now, those lovely eyes the color of a rain drenched
meadow. "I'll go make some coffee," he said, his voice
deep and uneven.

"He's such a kind man," Jeanne noted softly after he
had gone.

"He'll surely cry when his baby is born. He'll not be
able to keep his emotions buried then." Thomas snorted as
he gently cleaned the baby. "On the other hand, he's a
poker shark. Cares less if he takes the last dollar in my
pocket... Kylie, you and Michael are exhausted. Get some
rest."

"You'll be safe here," Kylie said as she straightened
Jeanne's bed and helped draw a clean gown onto her.

"You'll stay, too, won't you?"

"I'll stay." How many times had Michael and her
mother helped women like this?

Thomas's grin flashed in the shadows. "Too bad I didn't
catch you first, Kylie. The world could do with more hearts
like yours."

In his living room, Michael paced in front of the blazing
fire. He stopped to cross his arms in front of his chest and
frowned at her. "I love you and that's all there is to that."

Kylie poured herself onto the couch and sipped the tea
Michael had prepared. Now wasn't the time to sort out their
love. She wanted to come to him, free of the past, courting
him as he deserved. She would have truth running between
them, not the leashed, though magical, lovemaking of that
single, perfect night. Kylie smiled to herself, planning how
she would vamp him, and her smile grew as Michael's wary
frown deepened. "If you're set to argue," she said, stretching her body to watch the impact upon him, which was

perfect and hot and hungry, just as it should be. "I'm too tired. Come hold me."

His expression went blank, then he crossed to her, gently scooped her up in his arms and carried her into his bedroom, still mussed from their lovemaking. She held him tight as he lay beside her, drawing the covers over them and gave herself to sleep and the safety of Michael's arms.

For the next two weeks, she would come to Michael's arms every night. Lying tucked against him, returning his slow, thorough sweet kisses was enough. Throughout the nights, she and Michael took turns helping Jeanne. During the days, Soft Touches was heavily scheduled. Kylie worked very hard, keeping her lunch hour free to go to Michael, who always had lunch ready. In the evening, when she dragged herself home from Soft Touches, he was there to hold her, to tell her about Jeanne and the baby's progress.

Adept at cradling the baby in one arm and managing simple household tasks with his free hand, Michael surprised Kylie. He'd be a perfect father, she decided, stunned as he rocked the baby, cuddling him outrageously. Jeanne's recovery went well and in two weeks—on a mild December morning—Thomas returned to retrieve her. "Wanting to keep a closer eye on my patient," he'd said, with a merry twinkle in his eyes.

"How perfectly like Michael," Kylie muttered the next afternoon, for she was dressed for courting Michael and he was nowhere to be found. She touched the earrings and locket he'd given her as a teenager and wondered if he'd remember. Pausing to glance in his bedroom mirror, she tried to smooth her hair, the first of December wind and rain turning it into a wild, free mass framing her face. A touch of shadow deepened the blue of her eyes, a bit of buttery lip gloss made her lips seem fuller. A brush of a wand added color to her cheeks, though that color came natural enough when she thought of how she would love Michael, once his defenses were down. There would be no more holding himself away, leashing what ran deep and raw inside him. They were both exhausted once Jeanne left, and Michael had stayed away that night, leaving her alone in the bed they'd shared.

She'd had appointments to keep and couldn't hunt him down. Canceling her afternoon appointments had brought a few protests, but her clients were happy enough to re-schedule. She'd hurried to her mother's house, jerking the long forgotten dress from her closet. But Michael's house had been empty, the shower still beaded with water and smelling of soap and man.

"There will be no more of that, Michael Cusack," she murmured. Just as Thomas was driving away, she'd caught Michael's expression before he shielded it. The burning flick of his eyes told her of his passion; the hard lock of his body and the grim set of his lips said he was withdraw-ing behind his shields.

Unaccustomed to dresses and cosmetics, Kylie decided she'd done all she could with what she had. She hadn't been a man-hunter, but now one special man deserved hunt-ing and capturing. She fluttered her eyelashes at the woman in the mirror and smoothed the dress flowing tightly across her hips. Basic black and long sleeved, cut just above her knee, the dress was too much for the Wagon Wheel Café and the Silver Dollar. Still, her statement was important to make, an instinctive ritual for the woman wanting all of her love's attention. Kylie inhaled deeply and her eyes wid-ened at the deep vee at her chest. She tugged at the dress. "It's your fault, Michael, for feeding me so well. I'm not long and lithe at my best, but more packed and solid."

At the sound of hoofbeats, she peered out of the window. Michael bent against the chilling North wind, riding Jack into the barn. In the distance, his face was harsh, his hair pushed back from his fierce scowl. The brooding gray day, heavy with mist suited him, tearing her back to the night when he'd been so savage, efficiently dealing with the bully.

She had to run to him, tearing from the house, to hold him in her arms and keep him safe from his shadows.

Inside the barn, Michael unsaddled Jack. The wind swept through the barn, signaling an opened door. One glance at Kylie hurrying toward him, her eyes round and concerned, and Michael knew that he could easily hurt her. A loving woman, she should have more than a back alley fighter, scarred from life. He'd show her what he was and she'd turn away— "You should have worn a coat. You're shivering."

Michael tore off his coat, scented of him, and stuffed Kylie's arms into the sleeves, buttoning the front up to her throat. "Here, I want to show you my life," he said, snaring her wrist and tugging her to the stairs.

He wasn't meant for a pretty life, he decided as he punched in the key code that would open the upstairs bolted door. He tugged Kylie through and slammed the door shut behind them. Words rapped out of him, the dangerous life he'd led. "Bodyguard work, security for threatened politicians, communities, child retrieval, rescue work, safe installment, insurance and basic protection. I'm a silent partner in a company that manufactures and installs security devices. I test them—don't move until I turn off the alarms, or you'll take an electric jolt that will knock you on that fabulous backside. You can't see the detection beams. They're just there."

Michael tapped off the sensors that could painfully trap

an intruder. He leaned against the wall as she padded over the thick carpeting, meant to contain sound, to a wall lined with weapons. Sealed under glass, the armory was vicious and high tech. Sensor equipment lined another wall, dials and machines made to protect. Kylie's face was pale, her lips vivid against her skin, her eyes blue and rounded with the impact of his life. Messages purred off his fax machine, digital readings ran across another machine, and a computer blinked, waiting for a response.

Kylie looked like a fairy wandering amid a demon's lair, lightly touching as she passed. She turned to him and stripped away his coat. She kicked off her high heels as she stepped on his training mat. "Well, then, Michael Cusack. What am I to think? That you make a lot of money with these gizmos? Do you think that matters to me? Money?"

"This is what I am," he murmured, crossing to her, so that she would make no mistake. "I'm like my father, you see. Tough. You knew him. I could be like that eventually."

Her head went up and she sniffed delicately while surveying the walls lined with weapons. Then her blue eyes locked with his. "You think this will put me off, don't you?"

"It would most women." He couldn't stop his eyes from taking that raw, hungry stroll down her body, leaving him drooling. She was all woman, his woman, packed into a fragrant package of curves and— He remembered her body moving beneath his, over his, feminine and powerful and warm and lush. He swallowed roughly at the sight of her breasts, burgeoning from the deep vee. To keep from curving his hands around each softness to take it to his lips, Michael forced himself to breathe evenly, gathering his control. When he managed to pry his gaze upward, he found her smirking. She moistened her lips and slid him a sultry sidelong look. "Well?"

"Kylie, this is serious. Not playtime." Michael tried to force his hardened body to relax and failed. Kylie wasn't a woman to play games and clearly now, she was flirting with him. Who was she, this dazzling woman?

She tossed her hair and gave him the most feminine, appealing look he'd ever seen. "I know what I need to know. You asked for me. What did you say then? Did you mean it?"

He raked a hand through his hair and paced the length of the workout mat. "You know I did. We're about to be spread all over Sarafina Malagay's lovelorn newspaper column."

"So you think that will make me shiver, do you? Having Sarafina's nose in my love life?" Her hands shoved him from the back, jarring him. He pivoted, finding her snarling. "You think so little of me, Michael Cusack? You think all these gizmos and what you do—what you've done to survive—could stop what I feel, how my heart beats for you? You think this could stop me from loving you? Then go to hell."

He caught her before she could step off the mat, his arms circling her from behind. "Oh, sweetheart," he murmured as if the words were torn from his heart.

They were enough to tell her what she needed and Kylie turned in his arms. She gave him no chance to think, but locked her arms around him, fisting his hair. His mouth was hot and open on hers, tasting of hunger and passion and nights that would be long and satisfying. "You think too much, dear heart," she whispered, her eyes wide and blue upon him, her hand smoothing his cheek.

He wasn't thinking at all; he was straining to keep control. Amid the lethal gear of his life, Kylie was too untouched, too trusting. "Let's go into the house."

In the house, Michael paced in front of the fire he'd just stoked to life. "Aren't you going to say something about how I look, dear heart?" she asked carefully. "I'm asking you for a date—"

Then Michael's arms were around her, crushing her to him, his mouth hard and hungry over hers. "You drive me—" he said roughly against her cheek. "I'm trying to be Mr. Nice Guy and it isn't working. I thought we'd take time—"

The pounding of his heart told her that enough time had passed without him. "We both know what we want. Don't talk. Just feel."

She touched her ears, the gold studs gleaming in them, and the locket at her throat. "You gave me these. It doesn't matter, none of it, Michael. Just you and me, here together."

His finger prowled an earring, then circled her ear. "It's no gentle feeling in me now, Kylie, dear heart. Better step away and let me cool. I'd prefer to go slow and easy with you— You've got to understand—you're my rosebud, my angel and my torment all rolled into one perfectly curved, hand-fitting hot-blooded woman. It's hard for a man to adjust to all that—those big blue eyes eating him, that mouth tasting like forevermore and fire and heaven at the same time. How can you know what you mean to me, how you fill my heart and soul and how I don't know if I'm breathing or not until you're near? I can barely keep from— I can see you nursing our baby, holding that perfect little girl with blue eyes like yours against your breasts and nothing else makes any sense. You fascinate me, so feminine and sweet and caring. You're part fairy, part dream, and all woman with knowing, mysterious smiles that curl inside me, warming me. You move and my heart leaps, my hands tremble, and I wonder how could this marvelous creature want me? On the other hand, I'm quite greedy for you,'' his voice roughened and a fingertip strolled down between her breasts, ''when you touch me, I've only one thought—making love to you anywhere, anytime.''

She tried to swallow, tried to close her lips and couldn't. ''Is that how you feel about me?''

''Like I'd like to spend every minute with you for the rest of my life,'' he stated slowly, firmly. He looked away, his jaw set, the color rising on his cheeks. Then his dark green gaze flashed at her. ''I'm not taking it back, none of it. And that's that.''

''You haven't said anything about my dress, Michael.'' Who was this wonderful man, this lover she had taken to her heart and her body? How much more marvelous could life be? She wanted to hear more, to savor the wary way he gave his heart to her.

He rammed his hand through his hair, the trembling of it, telling of his deep emotions. ''It's the woman beneath that I love, and I'm wanting to take it off and hold you close and tight and naked against me. It's a need I fear I'll probably never lose. Just for you.''

As always, Kylie followed her instincts. With happiness blooming inside her, she leaped upon him, caught her arms around his shoulders and her legs around his narrow hips. Michael staggered back with the force, his hands finding and supporting her bottom. They burned her bare skin and Michael's head reared back, his green eyes widening. As he carried her down the hallway to his bedroom, one big hand slowly explored the garters running to her hose, found the snaps and released them as he shuddered, the heat between them growing. She nibbled at his bottom lip, and he

kissed the sensitive corner of hers. Then he tugged the back
zipper of her dress down and smoothed the silky skin beneath. Pressed so tightly against him, she barely felt the
black lace of her bra release. Then his mouth was open on
her, tugging and sending out hot waves to curl and lick at
her.

They fell onto the bed, Michael drawing away her clothing and then his, and then that one fierce look told her she'd
have everything. That she'd have the truth that ran between
them. Michael's hand slowly stroked down her side, pausing to cup and cherish her breast, to splay across her belly,
and to stroke her thighs, his eyes glittering above her, his
face taut with desire. "Oh, you're all woman, Kylie, dear
heart. Luscious and hot and fragrant."

Filled with happiness, she laughed out loud, and Michael
scowled down at her. "Well, you are," he stated as if she'd
challenged him.

He sucked in air roughly as she touched him, explored
him intimately. She read his desperation, felt it jar and mirror in her own body, and then as Michael's gaze flickered
down their bodies, hers pale against his rougher one, she
smoothed his chest and knew that his heart raced for her,
that his body lay hot and thrusting against hers. "I love
you, Michael," she whispered as his hands moved more
firmly upon her, cupping her, smoothing her upper thighs
as if he fought his need.

His mouth was on hers, taking greedily, hard and open
and slanting to fuse. She wrapped her arms around him,
locking him tightly against her as he moved over her and
that blunt pressure came into her moist, warm keeping. He
rocked gently upon her, her hips meeting his, as though
they were creating a tempo to last a lifetime. She dug her
fingers into his shoulders, nipped at his throat and Michael

trembled, his hands running down her legs, lifting them for a deeper fit. She took a breath, savoring the storm that would come tossing them against the pleasure. When she released it, the pleasure dived into her, Michael moving powerfully against her, but she met that power with her own, claiming him, feeding upon him. His kisses were wild now, feverish and packed with the raw need driving him. She fought him and herself, and then brought him home again, the rhythm so fast it hurled them into the storm, the tightening of her body matching his. Just out there, on that beautiful electrifying plane, time stood still, quivering, deliciously wrapped in pleasure. Fighting his body, trying to give her more, loving her desperately, the other part of his heart, his body, his soul, Michael knew that they were one.

His heart was her heart, filling her, pounding against her, as real and strong as a fiery brand, pouring into her, becoming one with her. Michael came slowly down to rest upon her, damp with the effort of holding himself, and the wild release that was taken out of his control. As she drifted in the aftermath of the storm, she smoothed his taut rippling back, his lips moved against her throat. "Dear heart," he murmured drowsily, as if he'd be saying that when they were years down the road of life. "I love you."

Michael grinned in the shadows of his barn, feeling boyish and powerful and macho and too lucky to be believed. The gift he'd chosen to give her wasn't flowers and jewelry, though he planned to give those, too. He studied his gift and his grin widened. There was just nothing like Kylie when she was courting. He never knew what to expect. The new ease between them had grown in the last week. He was a little dizzy with his love, still wary with the fit of it, but she'd asked him to the Last Dance of the Women's Council Christmas Dance. She'd be coming for him in a surrey, if the ground was clear of snow. If it wasn't, she'd borrow a sleigh.

They'd read Anna's journals together, and he'd held Kylie when she cried, missing her mother. She'd come to him, letting him hold her, giving her ease. Anna would be there, they both knew, loving them both and the children they would have. A strong woman, she'd given him the gift of a lifetime—Kylie.

Locked onto his future with Kylie, Michael moved quickly, selling his interest in the security company. He didn't want any part of that life now, didn't want it touching Kylie and the family they wanted to start soon. Other investments were chosen, and he'd purchased more land to raise cattle and goats and chickens and pigs. For his part, he wanted to raise their children, to see them play, to keep Kylie warm and happy and fed as she shared her gifts. He hadn't told her yet, but he wanted a brood filling their lives, wild happy children, just like Kylie had been.

As for the women Rosa Demitri and he tried to salvage, Kylie would hear nothing of Michael leaving his work. But realizing that Michael had paid more than his dues and needed time to enjoy his new life, Thomas White had arranged for another man, just as experienced, to help with the women needing protection, sharing their work. There would be times when Kylie's kind heart and healing ways would be needed, and Michael didn't begrudge that. It was her calling, a gift from her mother, and one needing to be shared.

The gift of the night vision glasses had purchased a measure of Karolina's wary trust and the Bachelor Club mourned losing another member.

Michael heard Kylie's footsteps coming closer, up to the upstairs room vacated of weapons and sensors. He didn't need electronic sensors to know that she was nearby; his body told him with a heady slam of happiness and hunger. He let the grin within him slide outside to a face once kept locked and cold. He let his happiness linger there, on the curve of his lips waiting to taste hers.

"Michael, can you help me move my hope chest to your house—?"

She closed the door, and slowly walked to him, blue eyes darkening as they ran down his denim jacket and jeans. He recognized that hot steaming look, his heart already pounding, his body hardening. "Hi, dear heart," she whispered, lifting on tiptoe to kiss him. She tasted of hunger and delight and dreams to come. "I'm home."

He turned her gently to view his gift in the center of the area. It gleamed boldly in the light, waiting for her. "Yum," Kylie said slowly, then turned back to Michael, her eyes alight. "I've always wanted a mechanical bucking bull."

"Land on the mat and take it slow," he warned firmly even as she began to undress.

"Yum," she whispered, moving into his arms. "In a bit, dear heart. In a bit."

Fidelity tapped her cane and looked out at the mid-December day, bright with promise. "Well, that's that. Michael Cusack and Kylie Bennett are going to be married. He rated an 'A plus' on the visit from the Committee for the Welfare of Brides. Oh, that boy will have her wearing a white gown and having a proper wedding right and good in Freedom's church. Anna would be so pleased. Well, girls, that is one of the Bachelor Club married, good and well. The Rules for Bride Courting have never failed, when done right. Has anyone heard if Kylie's sister, Miranda, is married yet? No one has heard? Well, find out! She'll be home for her sister's wedding and we don't want to miss our chance to marry off another one of the Bachelor Club.''

*   *   *   *   *

*Look for GABRIEL'S GIFT,
the next compelling romance in the*
FREEDOM VALLEY *series,*
*in April 2001
Also, don't miss Cait London's
fabulous 3-in-1 collection*
A TALLCHIEF CELEBRATION,
available in January 2001

MAN OF THE MONTH

For twenty years Silhouette has been giving
you the ultimate in romantic reads. Come join
the celebration as some of your favorite authors
help celebrate our anniversary with the most
sensual, emotional love stories ever!

Available at your favorite retail outlet.

Where love comes alive™

#1 *New York Times* bestselling author

NORA ROBERTS

brings you more of the loyal and loving,
tempestuous and tantalizing Stanislaski family.

Coming in February 2001

The Stanislaski Sisters

Natasha and Rachel

Though raised in the Old World traditions of their
family, fiery Natasha Stanislaski and cool, classy
Rachel Stanislaski are ready for a *new* world of love....

And also available in February 2001 from
Silhouette Special Edition, the newest book in the
heartwarming Stanislaski saga

CONSIDERING KATE

Natasha and Spencer Kimball's daughter Kate turns her
back on old dreams and returns to her hometown, where
she finds the *man* of her dreams.

Available at your favorite retail outlet.

Where love comes alive™

where love comes alive—online...

eHARLEQUIN.com

shop eHarlequin

- ♥ Find all the new Silhouette releases at everyday great discounts.
- ♥ Try before you buy! Read an excerpt from the latest Silhouette novels.
- ♥ Write an online review and share your thoughts with others.

reading room

- ♥ Read our Internet exclusive daily and weekly online serials, or vote in our interactive novel.
- ♥ Talk to other readers about your favorite novels in our Reading Groups.
- ♥ Take our Choose-a-Book quiz to find the series that matches you!

authors' alcove

- ♥ Find out interesting tidbits and details about your favorite authors' lives, interests and writing habits.
- ♥ Ever dreamed of being an author? Enter our Writing Round Robin. The Winning Chapter will be published online! Or review our writing guidelines for submitting your novel.

If you enjoyed what you just read,
then we've got an offer you can't resist!

Take 2 bestselling love stories FREE!

Plus get a FREE surprise gift!

COMING NEXT MONTH

#1339 TALL, DARK & WESTERN—Anne Marie Winston
Man of the Month
Widowed rancher Marty Stryker needed a wife for his young daughter, so he placed an ad in the paper. When attractive young widow Juliette Duchenay answered his ad, the chemistry between them was undeniable. Marty knew he was falling for Juliette, but could he risk his heart for a second chance at love and family?

#1340 MILLIONAIRE M.D.—Jennifer Greene
Texas Cattleman's Club: Lone Star Jewels
When Winona Raye discovered a baby girl on her doorstep, wealthy surgeon Justin Webb proposed a marriage of convenience to give the child a family. But for Winona, living under the same roof with the sexy doctor proved to be a challenge. Because now that Justin had the opportunity to get close to Winona, he was determined to win her heart.

#1341 SHEIKH'S WOMAN—Alexandra Sellers
Sons of the Desert
Anna Lamb woke with no memory of her newborn baby, or of the tall, dark and handsome sheikh who claimed to be her husband. Although she was irresistibly drawn to Ishaq Ahmadi, Anna couldn't understand his anger and suspicion until the sheikh revealed his identity...and his shocking reasons for claiming *her* as his woman....

#1342 THE BARONS OF TEXAS: KIT—Fayrene Preston
The Barons of Texas
Kit Baron was in serious trouble. One of her ranch hands was dead, and she was the only suspect. Then criminal lawyer Des Baron—the stepcousin Kit had always secretly loved— came to her rescue. Now he was determined to prove her innocence, but could Kit prove her love for Des?

#1343 THE EARL'S SECRET—Kathryn Jensen
When American tour guide Jennifer Murphy met the dashing young Earl Christopher Smythe in Scotland, sparks flew. Before long their relationship became a passionate affair and Jennifer fell in love with Christopher. But the sexy earl had a secret, and in order to win the man of her dreams, Jennifer would have to uncover the truth....

#1344 A COWBOY, A BRIDE & A WEDDING VOW—Shirley Rogers
Cowboy Jake McCall never knew he was a father until Catherine St. John's son knocked on his door. In order to get to know his son, Jake convinced Catherine to stay on his ranch for the summer. Could the determined cowboy rekindle the passion between them and persuade Catherine to stay a lifetime?

CMN1200